First Edition Paperback

ISBN: 978-0-6456898-1-5

I0587030

WHERE THE PINK

THE PINK

MEETS

THE BLUE

NEPTUNE HENRIKSEN

Content Notes

- Non-linear storyline

- Explicit sexual and BDSM scenes from the onset and throughout

- Discussion and reflection of a main character's current sobriety and past alcohol and party drug addiction (allusions to chemsex – the act of having casual sex while under the influence of illicit substances)

- Depictions, and mentions of, recreational illicit drug use

- Depiction, and themes of, self-harm

- Frequent and high impact course language from the onset and throughout

- Occasional allusions to, and use of, reclaimed queer language, slurs, and symbols

- Themes of internalised biphobia, self-loathing tied to queer identity, and strained feelings regarding queer sex (men having sex with men, male bisexuality)

- Themes of familial rejection, past familial abuse, and loneliness, because of queer identity

- Themes, and discussion of, the intersection between religion (cultural Christianity, Progressive/Reform Judaism) and sexuality

- Comparisons between queer sexuality, illicit drug use, and the divine and/or religious worship

- Themes of the intersection between class (and classism) and sexuality

- Background of, and brief allusions to, historical, political, and global events between the years 2016 and 2020, both years inclusive

Part 1

In My Office?

After Hours Ok For You?

Lu <3
Thu 16/08/18 17:14
ready to go? all clear here 👀

Stephen From Work
Thu 16/08/18 17:14
still on hk call. prob 10 min

Lu <3
Thu 16/08/18 17:15
ok waitinggg 😁

Stephen From Work
Thu 16/08/18 17:23
omw 🐍

Part 2

It's So Random
Of Us To Be
In Your Office Right Now!!

Lucas is once again looking his green, pleading, wanton eyes, up to Stephen, mouth full of cock.

His calves and thighs burning, as he squats before Stephen, hands on Stephen's hips, hard cock invading his throat vigorously.

Stephen looks down at him, watching Lucas's needy eyes, as they communicate the hope that his effort is satisfactory.

His pleas soon answered.

"Uh, yeah... th-that's fucking g-good, Watterson..." Stephen praises, his American accent holding curses differently, more punctuated and harsh, in the dark office.

That harshness spat those words right down to Lucas, as Stephen's brown eyes bore into Lucas's libidinous gaze.

Lucas letting out a whimper, vibrating through Stephen's dick, a moan leaving his lips in turn, as he throws his head back in ecstasy.

"Oh yeah, you love being used don't you, bitch?" Stephen spits, rocking his head forward, watching Lucas' fiery desire.

Such passion, such eagerness, positively dripping from Lucas, as he focuses only on providing pleasure.

Stephen's hands firmly around Lucas' head, his fingers laced in short salt-and-pepper hair, as he watches Lucas' cherry blossom lips becoming plump and slick.

Another whimper reverberating through Stephen's cock, Lucas squeezing his grip on Stephen's hips, two encouraging responses to this act of degradation.

"You're s-so good for me, Watterson..." Stephen praises, his words rasping as he edges closer with each thrust.

Lucas's eyes widen, the praise pulsing through him, exactly the words to swarm his system, lighting up the beautiful, evasive, spots, floating in the nebulous high, shooting salvation through his nerves.

A twitch in his underwear, reminding him just how loudly his own cock screams for attention, remaining hard and untouched under his dress pants.

The unfairness if it all, Lucas knowing he won't be touched, only here to provide release, then be left, glorious and perverse. Amplifying the tightness in his trousers, and the wet patch he can feel at the tip.

Stephen tightens his grip on Lucas' hair, pulling him off, Lucas gasping for air in turn, eyes fixed on Stephen. Dazed, lost, foggy.

"You want me to cum down your fucking throat, Watterson?" Stephen asks, cock tip resting on Lucas' plump, pink lips, hot breath caressing the underside.

With eyes half-closed, breath ragged, heart racing, Lucas nods.

"What was that?" Stephen teases, his cock twitching against Lucas' face.

Lucas reaches his tongue out, trying to speak without words.

"I said... What was that?" Stephen asks again, guiding the lustful and squirming Lucas away from his hard cock.

Lucas grips tighter into Stephen's thighs, his own absolutely screaming for rest, more alight than his yearning, as he hangs on the tripping point, his balance precarious, on the very balls of his feet, behind his own desk, in the pitch-black Melbourne winter evening.

"Y-yes... yes please! S-Sir!" Lucas calls, his English accent almost completely lost in his dizzy tone, deep in his favourite place.

Stephen looks down, his soft, dark, curls sticking to his glistening forehead, breath thick, as he guides Lucas back just enough to again rest his cockhead between those pink lips.

"Yes... what?" Stephen teases, his tone playful but dominant. "Yes please... what?"

"Y-yes please, Sir... Pl-please c-cum down my..." Lucas breathes, his words floating up to Stephen, as he swims in his own red-hot longing. "my th-throat... I-I want to feel... it."

Watching Lucas in such a daze, looking up at him with those pleading green eyes, it was enough to make Stephen cum untouched. But he's kind enough to fulfill Lucas' request.

In a swift move, Stephen pushes Lucas onto his cock, firm and controlled, the sensation of the tip hitting the back of Lucas' throat, after such respite, flooding bliss through his system, eliciting a moan from Stephen's apricot lips.

Lucas moans in kind, relishing in being nothing more than a thing, savouring the thrill of being used, lost in a space between this realm and the next.

Those moans sending vibrations through Stephen's cock, up his spine, as he fucks Lucas' mouth, release approaching, closer, nearer, right there.

"Ah f-fuck, I-I'm gonna cum, Watterson!" Stephen calls, his words bouncing around the small, dark office.

Lucas can only watch, keen and taken, his throat full of Stephen's cock, his hair full of Stephen's hands, his ears filling with Stephen's ecstasy, his own cock untouched and wanting in his trousers.

Stephen looks down once more, seeing Lucas looking up at him like he's the embodiment of sex, sin, and devotion, as though he's worshipping at the altar of desire.

It's enough to send Stephen over the edge, his head rolling back, euphoria washing over him, delicious sounds pulsing out of him, engulfing Lucas' office in

Stephen's deep, lewd, moans, echoing around them, a chorus of elation.

Shivers running up his spine, his head spinning, his breaths ragged, his hot cum spilling down Lucas' throat, his cock twitching, once, twice, three times, four times.

Coming back to Earth, he slowly pulls Lucas off his cock, taking in short breaths in the aftershocks.

Stephen keeping his grip firm of the back of Lucas's head, tilting the face up to see how flushed and depraved Lucas looks, as though he'd move the sun and the planets just to have Stephen's cock down his throat again.

"F-fuck, you look good like th-that, Watterson." Stephen praises, tracing fingers over Lucas's cheek and running a thumb along his soaked, plump lips.

"Th-thank you, Mr. Herzig." Lucas replies, breathless and electrified, his entire body ablaze with desire and pent-up sexual energy.

"I bet you'd like a little-" Stephen tightens his grip on that salt-and-paper hair, tilting Lucas back ever so. "slap right about now."

"Oh, pl-please, yes... Y-yes yes please, Sir." Lucas begs, vibrating with need.

Stephen pulls his caressing hand back, Lucas eyes following his movements with palpable anticipation, and swings hard, slapping firmly against Lucas' eager face.

"Thank y-"

Lucas thanks are interrupted by Stephen's back hand against his other cheek, the sensation welcome, but taking him by surprise, his legs shaking in response.

"T-thank you, sir!" Lucas calls, a whimper following his words, as the stings resonate through his over-stimulated body.

"Such a good little slut for me." Stephen praises, running his hands from Lucas's hair, up clinging arms, feeling hot skin through a sage green shirt, and pausing at Lucas' hands. "Now clean yourself up."

Stephen's hands slipping under Lucas's fingers, as they fight to stay gripped on hips, the bolt keeping the hinge connected, and with a swift move, pulling them apart.

A whimper leaves Lucas' lips, as he falls ungracefully, struggling to catch himself with his palms, scrambling up onto his forearms, legs spent and aching, flopped out in front of him, trying to steady his breath, feeling his pulse in his rock-hard cock.

The silence screams through the small office, as Stephen steps away, and Lucas watches, not daring to move or speak, unsure if he'd be given permission to touch himself or not, and still awaiting, or hoping, for more praise.

Without a word, Stephen tucks his glossy cock back in his boxer briefs, and takes his time slipping into his trousers, undershirt, and dress shirt, feeling Lucas' salacious eyes on him, waiting and eager.

Mercifully, Stephen turns to Lucas, dripping with anticipation, as Stephen leans over him, speaking into the quiet.

"When I leave..." Stephen instructs, hushed, yet commanding and intense. "You can get yourself off. But I want you here again next Friday. That mouth of yours is fucking good."

He lets out a deep, desperate moan, but is cut off by Stephen bobbing down and taking him in for a rough and passionate kiss.

Lucas' hands remaining glued to the floor, not daring to touch without permission, as Stephen runs his fingers through Lucas' hair, down his neck, over his shoulders, conquering, yet gentle, wanting to explore, to feel.

Stephen tasting himself on Lucas' tongue, salty and familiar, feeling the absolute desperation coursing through Lucas, as he kisses back with zeal, like holy deliverance is contained within Stephen's lips.

Stephen pulls back slowly, Lucas following him, eyes still closed, hoping for more of that exhilarating kiss.

But as Lucas' eyes open, they see Stephen putting on his suit jacket, and grabbing his backpack and winter coat, before turning off the desk light, and heading out the door of Lucas's office; a sliver of light streaming in, and swiftly fading, leaving Lucas in the completely dark room alone, to finally release his own tension.

Part 3

Nothing Like Bumping Into

A Colleague After Hours

Stephen clicks the door closed, finding himself in the bright hallway, his eyes needing a moment to adjust, the past few moments still playing in his mind's eye, as he throws on his coat, picks up his backpack, before powerwalking down the empty corridor.

Reliving Lucas' devoted green eyes locking on his, he bites his lip, feeling the wetness that had been left by that final kiss.

Hastily, he rummages through his pockets for a tissue, should he run into someone.

Try as he might, his rummaging is fruitless, and with more worry coursing through his veins with each passing second, he relents to wiping his lips on the sleeve of his coat, and trying to rub the wetness out, just in case someone else is here.

And then, as if manifested by his anxieties, he rounds the corner to bump right into Holly.

"Oh hey!" She pipes up, Occa accent thick, as she is equally surprised by Stephen's late-night presence, as he is hers. "What, did ya forget something, New York?"

Holly looks him over, dark eyes squinting behind darker, thick lashes, full lips pouting curiously.

"No- Ah, I mean, yes- I did forget my... I, like..." Stephen stumbles, Philadelphia affectation seeping in, chewing his words, affecting vowels, as he struggles to think of why someone would be here at this hour.

"No worries, hun." Holly cuts in, giving Stephen a friendly tap on the arm. "I won't tell the boss." She continues, before walking past a still-off-guard Stephen. "Mainly because I don't fucking care!"

Her words echo back to Stephen, as she saunters down the corridor, waving as she goes, unseen by a frozen Stephen.

He snaps out of his swimming thoughts, another anxiety rushing in, and turns quickly to look behind him, wondering if Holly was going into the only office that was still occupied.

He stares in silent horror as he realises, he's unfortunately correct.

A breathless Lucas has his knuckles in his teeth, with the other hand feverishly bringing himself closer. His face hot, his mouth tasting of cum, as he hides under his own desk, scrunched up, in absolute darkness.

A click at the door causes him to freeze in place. Was Stephen back? That wasn't something they did. So, it was someone else? At this time? What would anyone want in his office right now?

He is somewhat safe in his spot, which couldn't really be seen from the door. But he remains absolutely still all the same.

The overhead light goes on, and Lucas can feel his heartbeat in his crimson cheeks.

A presence humming to themself as they rummage around, causing the seconds to stretch so tight, they could break at any moment.

Lucas feeling exposed, foolish, and so fucking turned on, knowing one more pump was all he'd need. But opting instead to remain paused in this pumping, and bite down further on his own knuckle, relishing in the mix of tension and pain.

Sweat glistening, surrounding him with the strong, refreshing, smell of tea tree, as his deodorant works overtime.

Finally, the sound of the presence picking something up, declaring a soft victory to themself, and footsteps moving to the door, the light switch flicking off, leaving Lucas in darkness, as the unknown someone clicks the door open, accompanied by the soft squeak of the door hinge, all quietly telling Lucas he wasn't alone just yet. But very nearly.

Lucas counts down the milliseconds until he hears that door click behind the presence, the overwhelming lust slowing time down, with Lucas having only the option of griping tighter on his hot red cock, as the moment teases him with solitude and bliss.

The click comes and so did Lucas, only one pump, and he is riding the pulses of rhapsody.

He quickly grips his own throat, his mouth agape, his pulse rushing against his fingers, trying his best to remain as quiet as possible.

Spurting his release, eyes slamming shut, as he remembers Stephen's firm hands around his head, using Lucas like he was nothing more than a fuck toy, just what he lives for.

Three. Four. Five. And he's gasping, rocking forward, his pleasure fading, his body exhausted.

He looks to the mess he's made in his dress trousers, and knows whatever he has in the office won't get that out, but he'll try for an hour anyway.

Part 4

Good Fucking Morning,
Babes!

"How's ya head?" Holly asks, falling into stride with Stephen, reusable mug in hand.

"My- my- what?" Stephen stutters, feeling hot under his wool coat, and not just because of the central heating.

"You were here late too, so… you had drinks and came back, or…?" Holly clarifies.

Taking a sip from her mug, and sighing to herself, enjoying the sweet wonder of coffee, she looks to Stephen, awaiting an answer. Her dark, ringlet curls, bouncing as she tilts her head to him.

"Oh! Yeah, my head's fine…" Stephen fumbles, blushing under the heat, looking as guilty as sin. "I didn't- didn't, like… have… too many."

"Alright New York, no one's grilling you here." Holly playfully reassures, simultaneously dismissive and caring, as only Australians are. "Just talking some shit while my brain warms up, aye."

And with that, she gives Stephen a little nudge with her elbow, and breaks off, making her way to the office kitchen.

Usually, Stephen would walk right past that small, fluorescent-lit, white-walled room, but he spots someone in there that he'd recently emptied his balls into. And look! That someone is making his usual green tea.

"Lucas! Morning." Stephen calls, following Holly into the kitchen.

"Good, um… Good morning, Stephen! M-morning Holly." Lucas replies, guilt behind the eyes, even this early in the day.

Those guilty eyes are busy as all hell, frantically looking from Holly to Stephen, trying to decipher what was going on between the two of them just moments before.

Stephen sees it, but it's unnoticed by Holly, as she plops her backpack on the kitchen counter, and takes out her packed lunch.

"Oh, so he gets a 'good morning', and I only get a 'morning', do I?" Holly jokes, turning back to Lucas, lunchbox in one hand, the other on her hip in faux-indignation. "What are ya… sucking his dick or something?"

Lucas gives out a strained laugh, Stephen trying to follow, as they look from each other to Holly, and back again, while she's rooting around in the fridge. Their silent exchange unseen.

"I'm not saying that because New York is bi, I'm saying that because I'm a cunt." Holly muses, continuing her fridge search. "So, if you're gunna go to HR about it, make sure they know it's because I'm a certified cunt. Got the paperwork and every-"

As Holly lifts her head from the fridge, she cuts herself off, observing the tension between Lucas and Stephen.

"Oh shit, I'm sorry you two, I took that one too far…" Holly apologises, her body language completely deflating. "was it the 'cunt', New York? I know you yanks can be sensitive."

"No, no it was ok, like, and I'm all for… like, reclaiming… that word, but…"

"It's a bit early for the dick-sucking jokes." Lucas swoops in, able to match Holly's brash blueness, and saving Stephen from his own loss for words. "I only start my dick-sucking jokes at ten a.m., and my pussy-eating jokes at ten-thirty."

Holly looks at Lucas for a beat, then bursts into laughter, reaching for the fridge door to steady herself. Her broad cackles bouncing around the tiny office kitchen.

Lucas and Stephen looking at each other nervously, surrounded by Holly's laughs, feigning chuckles themselves, hoping this moment will soon pass.

"That's a fucking good one, London." Holly praises, emphasising her words with a point to him, before closing the fridge and reaching for her backpack. "See you two in the nine-thirty."

Stephen and Lucas make small sounds of agreement, the stiff atmosphere either continuing to go unnoticed by Holly, or perhaps not something she concerns herself with.

Holly slings her backpack over her shoulder, sauntering out of the kitchen, leaving Stephen and

Lucas waiting in pointed silence, absolute statues, listening for when Holly's footsteps fade.

"Ste, what the fuck was that?" Lucas shout-whispers, an unexpected sharpness seeping through, usually not heard in his Midlands accent. "It's like she *knows*. I told you we should stick to Fridays."

"She doesn't, at least not from me." Stephen defends, matching Lucas' shout-whisper, despite deflating in his spot.

"Because I thought I made it clear that it's *just* sexual, and that we're-"

"Keeping it quiet. Yeah Lu, I got it, ok?" Stephen interrupts, avoiding Lucas' eyeline, and choosing to look at the ghost-white tiled floor.

"I didn't- it's not... I just..." Lucas stumbles, now aware he's hit a nerve, scrambling for words and absolution. "Sorry, that's my stuff, and... um..."

"You know... we can always... talk about that 'stuff'?" Stephen offers, wishing he could actually know the man he's had an arrangement with for several months.

"Yeah... um maybe, y-you know... I sh-should get to the nine-thirty." Lucas avoids, grabbing his green tea, and hurrying out of the kitchen.

Stephen heaves a heavy sigh, watching Lucas go for a moment, thoughts running through his head.

With another huff, he takes off his backpack dropping it down, and takes off his coat, sliding it down his shoulders, and folding it over his arm, leaning back against the kitchen wall, and taking a second to feel the frustration at this incomplete relationship he's been wading through for months.

There is something so crucial missing, that nurturing element, aftercare and pillow talk, even just eating takeaway together.

This thing is intriguing, sure, but it takes its toll in moments like this.

Part 5

Let's Talk

About Feelings, Ba-by

"I... I think I'm... I'm actually n-not happy with this an-anymore..." Lucas mumbles, his calves aching once again.

He rocks back onto the floor, the come down hitting him hard. All he'd thought about all week was being here again, sinking into the liminal space of submission, being taken, being had. All he's yearned for was another hit of this, so delicious, so moreish, beautiful and tragic, running through his veins.

And now he's had it. He's crashing down. Everything flooding back.

All the haunting thoughts. Pushed down with sex. As usual.

Still breathless, still untouched, still cherry-lipped. But this is unlike every other office visit.

Stephen watches him, taking in his words, hearing what he's asking for, hoping to offer something of value.

"I'd... love to... reciprocate." Stephen tries, his tone returning to tender through ragged breaths.

He's still standing over Lucas, shirt unbuttoned, softening cock out, catching his breath, leaning against Lucas' desk.

"That's not..." Lucas pushes back.

He's falling so hard, so fast, feeling exposed and powerless, and not in the way he enjoys.

"Shit... Lu... what's...?" Stephen worries, zipping up and bobbing down to Lucas's level.

Settling into place, Stephen pops one knee up, chin resting on it, face glistening in the light of the warm desk lamp. How it catches his olive skin beautifully, illuminating his faded freckles, the winter muting them, as August barrels on. His brown eyes so caring, like he's capable of seeing the wonder in anything, open to every happiness.

But Lucas can barely look at him, his focus turning to the carpet, as he crosses his legs, holding his ankles, slumping forward. Trying his best to fold over completely, hoping to hide from such warm eyes.

"It's not the... I like the, uh... d-dynamic." Lucas clarifies, shrugging. "It's just- w-what if we... tried other things... and, um... other... pl-places?"

His words drifting over to Stephen. Surprising, but incredibly welcome. A long-held hope coming to fruition. Even so, that surprise was front of mind in Stephen's reply.

"I thought you- I mean, are you sure? Last time we talked, you said-"

"It's been so good of y-you to be... so... a-and it's been, y'know... really good, because I couldn't, um... handle more, then." Lucas mumbles, small and ashamed, his words only for Stephen to hear. "But, I think I wan- I think I *need* a little more... now. What do you... th-think about that?"

"I... would love to." Stephen beams, his voice loving, his kindness ever present. "Like, I've been hoping we could... sorta like... expand things, but I've been really wary of, like, pushing you... before you are... sorta like, fully ready."

"Oh." Lucas realises.

Previous conversations replaying in a moment. Stephen trying, slowly, gently, to offer small steps here and there, hoping to softly coax Lucas out of his shell.

But of course, Lucas has put those away somewhere unknowable, fooled himself into a false conclusion, one that was now being shattered before his eyes.

"Well, I've... I think I've sort of..." Lucas mumbles, unfurling enough to look to a waiting, open, Stephen. "I've worked through some of that... b-because of... um, you."

"Lucas..." Stephen glows, his hand over his heart, smile dancing across his face. "Could I...?"

Lucas answers silently, tentative smile on his face, as he pushes up to his knees, shuffling over, closing the gap between the two.

Stephen beams, taking Lucas into a tight and loving embrace, feeling Lucas's heartbeat against his, Lucas's chin nuzzling into his neck, Lucas's breath on the top of his spine.

Nearer and nearer Stephen holds him, moving into his space, until there is nothing between them, relishing in such closeness.

Slow, real, present.

Lucas savours Stephen's touch, silently cursing himself for keeping Stephen at arm's length all these months, denying himself something so natural, so simple, so connecting, along the way.

Stephen's arms around him, broad and strong, so reassuring, like nothing could hurt him, not here.

Something deep inside Lucas screams in relief, a fragment untouchable by hours of gay porn, unreachable by all the time spent with a cock in his mouth, unscratchable by any other means than simple, tender, touch.

All Lucas can do is close his eyes and take as much of this feeling in as he's able.

Breathe in. Breathe out. Welcome this.

Be here, be now, in his arms.

Stephen feels something twitch, and Lucas' eyes fly open, suddenly busy.

"Oh." Stephen remarks, feeling Lucas's ready cock against his thigh.

"Well, yes... don't worry about that-"

"What if I... did?" Stephen interrupts, flirty as ever, pulling back just enough to look Lucas in the eye. "Or is that too much, too soon?"

Lucas' pale face goes beetroot red, another twitch giving him away, nowhere to hide.

"No... I mean, yes." Lucas stumbles, trying to trust himself and his desires, as though that isn't the boulder to his hill. "No, it's not too soon, yes I would... like very much if you..."

"If I sucked your dick, Watterson?" Stephen teases, completing Lucas' sentence for him.

Lucas nods small and vigorous, as though any larger gestures would be heard, by some silent peripheral eyes, ambiguous, but ever-present.

But he's going to say yes, this time, he will push that boulder up the hill, even if it might go rolling back down tomorrow. Tonight is for delight, and tomorrow can fuck right off.

Stephen brings a hand up to Lucas' forehead, tracing soft touches from the top of his face, down to his cheek, and under his chin, resting a thumb gently just under his bottom lip.

Lucas relishes in the touch wordlessly, a blessing of divine sensation, opening himself up to something so long denied.

Stephen guides Lucas in, and finally, thankfully, their lips touch.

He tastes himself on Lucas' lips and tongue, familiar now, but always enjoyed. His fingers reaching up to the back of Lucas' head, pulling in closer, deeper, to fall into his essence and energy, enjoying the pent-up emotion that radiates out of him. Another bite of Stephen's favourite treat.

He traces kisses along Lucas's jaw, down the neck, gentle and slow, caressing his lips along the sensitive nape.

Whimpers fall from Lucas' lips, his body on fire, like never before, original and beautiful, feeling new pleasures, as fresh pedals open, a flower in bloom.

Stephen continues caressing kisses up to Lucas's ear, biting tenderly on his earlobe, eliciting a moan that radiates through Lucas' entire chest.

"Then you..." Stephen whispers, commanding and provocative. "You better ask fucking nicely for it, bitch."

A tingle runs through Lucas in an instant, causing his hips to buck against Stephen's, melting into the magic.

"P-please, Sir..." Lucas breathes, through strained moans. "Please... w-would you... pl-please... s-suck my cock, Mr. Herzig... I've- I've been such a good boy."

"You have been a good boy." Stephen coos into Lucas's neck. "And I want to make you cum, I really do."

He dances a hand down Lucas's body, controlled and teasing, feeling heat under fingers, pausing just at Lucas' belt buckle.

"But it's so hard to tell if you want me to, Lu."

"Urgh!" Lucas calls out, digging his nails into his own palms. "S-Sir... pl-please... would you please, p-please... m-make me cum... I-I need it so much... Sir, p-please..."

Stephen pulls back just enough to really take Lucas in.

His breathing ragged, face glistening, body shaking with anticipation.

"You're so fucking beautiful when you're worked up, slut." Stephen praises, yanking suddenly on Lucas' belt buckle, causing another jolt of the hips, and eliciting a shudder from Lucas. "Now... Lay. Down."

Stephen pulls his hands away from Lucas, a sudden, commanding movement, causing another majestic moan from Lucas, enjoying the thrill of submission, the beauty in surrendering completely.

He falls back, hands by sides, knees up, feet planted. Looking up at a towering Stephen, a familiar and delectable sight.

That towering figure guiding Lucas' hands above, a silent command this where they are to remain. Lucas glancing up, agreeing without words.

Stephen traces fingers along Lucas' palms, down dress-shirt-covered forearms, along heaving sides, and up to raised knees, guiding them down. Showing, not telling. Dominance in gentle touch.

He draws teasing fingers up Lucas' thighs, pressing and squeezing, feeling the burning desire under the Merino wool, and delighting in Lucas' incoherent pleading.

Those commanding, deviant hands, reaching the brown leather belt, tracing his index finger over the buckle, causing a quick string of 'please, fuck, fuck, fuck' from Lucas' plump lips, as he watches in anguished bliss.

Stephen locking eyes with Lucas, who looks about ready to explode, in every sense, as Stephen dances his fingers along the leather, around, and down, to tuck under both sides of Lucas' hips, holding firmly.

Lucas watches with a mix of quiet confusion, and even quieter thrill, so incredibly taken and desired.

Stephen enjoys every second of Lucas' responses, raising an eyebrow as he leans into Lucas' belt, and bites down on it, pulling slowly, as he presses down his thumbs on Lucas' hips, holding the brown leather in place on either side, as deliberately, tantalisingly, he pulls the belt through its gold loop, adding a little toss of his curls, as the strap springs free, watching Lucas all the while.

An impassioned Lucas letting out a number of curses, words of thanks, and delirious pleas, at the sight, before rolling his head back, unable to watch much more of the teasing, or so he thinks.

"Nu-uh..." Stephen teases, tucking his fingers into the sides of Lucas' trousers. "You know I've **got** to watch you."

Stephen waits for Lucas to steady his breathing, enough to follow instructions, giving Stephen his full attention, as he watches tucked fingers skim along the inside of his waistband, the sight enough to have him whimpering again, and the sensation sending tingles all along his hips.

"P-please, Sir!" Lucas calls out, his words bouncing around the room, louder than his moans and whimpers, cradling the pair in echoes of pleading.

"All you had to do was ask, bitch." Stephen muses, bathing in Lucas' desire, smirking fiendishly.

All at once, Stephen slips the buckle open, unzips Lucas's dress trousers, and pulls down the boxer briefs under them, to have Lucas's devil-red dick in his grasp.

"Eyes on me, Watterson." Stephen demands, voice low and firm.

Lucas does as he's told, watching helplessly as Stephen locks eyes with him, and extends a tongue, licking from the base, slowly, teasingly, to the sensitive tip, curling that tongue at the top, tasting the remnants of the pooling arousal, and closing his lips around the cockhead.

Delighting in Lucas' low, desperate moans, as they layer into a glorious symphony, falling completely into Stephen's temptations. Waiting, hoping, for more, just a little more, any moment now.

As if able to hear Lucas' silent hopes, Stephen grips fingers into hips, parts his lips, enveloping that cock in one quick move, feeling the tip hit the back of his throat, and looking ferociously into Lucas' eyes.

It's unexpected. Causing ungodly sounds from Lucas, unprepared for the divinity, a slew of thanks falling from his cherry blossom lips.

Stephen holds Lucas's length deep in his throat, keeping his eyes locked on Lucas as he lets out a steady, low hum, sending luscious vibrations through Lucas' entire being.

The glory of the tantalising vibrations, leaving Lucas letting out the most beautiful sounds, as he sinks into the feeling, riding the waves of pleasure.

Stephen pulls back a little for air, the sudden breath on Lucas' wet cock, sending shivers up his spine, as more moans escape his lips, completely present in the moment, not thinking of a present or a past, simply swimming in the delight of the now.

Then, without warning, Stephen is vigorously fucking his throat on Lucas, fast and deep, leaving Lucas to call out a thousand words of thanks, gripping even tighter on the carpet. Taken, conquered, floating in ecstasy.

Lucas's sounds grow more beautiful, strained, and desperate with each thrust, circling around the pair in the small dark office, louder and bolder with each thrust, until Lucas is boring his gaze deep into Stephen's eyes, biting his lip, and nodding hastily.

It was all the warning Stephen needs, as he delights in watching Lucas throw his head back, and takes in the almighty view of a man completely lost in the most heavenly escape.

Lucas' fingers white on the carpet, as he feels the miraculous ascending his body, the pulses ravaging his being, twitching once, twice, three times, then four, his face scrunching, his gorgeous declarations filling his office.

Stephen watches.

Absorbing, treasuring, devouring.

Hot, heavy, sacred.

Immersed in Lucas' calls of euphoria, feeling the release spill deep down his throat, as Lucas positively shakes beneath him.

The salacious sounds fade, replaced with ragged breaths, and Stephen slowly pulls off, sucking all the way up, wanting to taste as much as he can.

Lucas floating back down to Earth, his vision going in and out of focus, his fingers tingling as he finally relaxes his grip.

"Now, why would you deprive me of that?" Stephen asks, smiling up at a half-coherent Lucas. "You were absolutely... beautiful."

Lucas chuckles, a little embarrassed, a little flattered, mostly orgasm-high.

"I, uh... I w-would have th-thought..." Lucas answers, hiding his flushed face in the crook of his elbow. "That, um, was... obvious..."

"Obvious how?" Stephen asks, sitting up on his knees, grabbing some tissues from Lucas's desk.

"Y'know..." Lucas mumbles, still hiding.

"I... obviously don't... is it, like, sorta... an English thing?" Stephen prods, wiping his mouth and chin, and placing the used tissues in the bin under Lucas's desk.

"Fuck off, Herzig." Lucas jokes, a smile on his lips, despite his unseen eyes. "I'm not a walking cliché!"

"Mainly because you're laying down."

Lucas answers that remark with a raised middle finger from his free hand, as he remains hidden behind his elbow.

"If this is too much too soon, I can drop it, Lu." Stephen reassures, his tone warmer, as he sits down beside Lucas.

Finally, Lucas moves his arm, looking Stephen in the eye, with a vulnerability and shame that stings Stephen in an all-too-familiar place.

"It's… sexuality shit." Lucas admits, looking down at his now flaccid, and very much exposed, cock.

"I mean… that's something I could, you know, maybe understand." Stephen half-jokes, giving a head tilt, and a hand flourish.

"Yeah… I guess so." Lucas muses, pushing himself up enough to reach for his underwear and trousers.

"Oh sorry, did you want a-" Stephen asks, gesturing toward the tissues.

"Yeah, go on." Lucas answers, sitting up, and immediately hunching over.

"So… orientation shit?" Stephen asks, reaching up to the desk, and handing Lucas the box.

"It's, y'know…" Lucas begins, dabbing himself with the tissues, physically and emotionally bare. "If I don't let the guy touch me, then…"

"Mmm, gotcha." Stephen nods, sitting up fully, but staying just behind Lucas' eyeline, purposefully present, yet unseen.

"And it's not like I'm, um… completely ashamed." Lucas continues, pulling up his underwear and trousers, feeling at least physically covered. "It's, um… whatever… but it's also y'know…"

"The act itself is… sorta…" Stephen again nods, trailing off, then clarifying when Lucas looks back at him in confusion. "Like… wrong, sinful, disgusting, to'eivah, like… take your pick."

Lucas silently agrees, scooching back a little to fully face Stephen, and look deep into those sincere, loving, brown eyes, barely believing someone can be so self-aware and somehow not be crushed by the weight of that awareness. It was never a balance Lucas could strike.

"I mean…" Stephen elaborates, hoping to finally explore more of each other. "Among Progressive Judaism it's all-"

"Kosher?" Lucas interrupts, a cheeky smile on his face.

"Shut the actual fuck up." Stephen retorts, giving Lucas a playful push. "Sure. It's kosher, Lu. Thank you for that. That was really great." Stephen sarcastically nods, then takes in a refreshing breath, and continues. "Anyway, it's like… with Conservative and Orthodox communities it's like… shall we say, a different story sometimes…"

Stephen trails off, making a face of exasperation that Lucas knows well.

"Yeah… fuck." Lucas nods. "My parents are those odd culturally Christian types where they say they're not actually religious, and they say they're open and accepting of everyone, but I've never really come out to them, because…"

Lucas trails off, trying to even find words for something he tries to lock out of his mind so often, like trying to see colours he's continually told couldn't possibly exist.

Stephen sees it, he extends a hand out, palm up, waiting in between their bodies, a lifeboat approaching a sinking ship.

The boat waits, patient and calm, until Lucas closes the gap, and places his hand in Stephen's, somewhere between romance and comfort. A shared breath. Relief. Strength to push on.

"Because... well, I often ask myself... how much of that will actually be true?" Lucas continues, rubbing his thumb over Stephen's wrist. "It's like... there was always this question of... what would they genuinely do if I did tell them? Or fuck, brought a bloke home?"

Stephen breathes a sigh of recognition. Something so universal, even if it wasn't his reality, he knows it's sting.

"Sorry, fuck!" Lucas cuts through, ashamed to have taken up so much air with his ramblings. "What is your family like? Sorry."

"No need to apologise." Stephen comforts, squeezing Lucas' hand. "I like hearing about you. It's nice."

Words can't come to Lucas, to be confronted by such steadiness, such genuine interest, such patience, he can barely process it.

"But if you wanna know..." Stephen begins, shaking Lucas from his cloud of silence. "Do you... wanna know?"

Lucas nods, smiling, hoping to understand how Stephen can be... so very Stephen.

"Cool." Stephen smiles, running his thumb over Lucas' knuckles. "I mean, I'm very fortunate, and like, I know that, but yeah, my parents are wonderful. But it's a little hard to talk to them right now, which... like, it is what it is."

Lucas deflates at Stephen's words, and it's seen, felt too.

"But! This is to say, that they like, actually walk the walk." Stephen tries to catch Lucas' evasive eyeline as he continues, Philly accent seeping into his sincere words. "Which hey, if you're gonna call yourselves Progressive, you'd hope so, but... yeah. Although... maybe that's just because I have, like, three sisters, and one of them is also queer. She sorta, like... paved the way."

"Oh."

Lucas continues to evade Stephen's gentle checks, looking away whenever he feels Stephen's attempts to make eye contact, trying to process anything that's being said. So familiar, yet foreign, and not just because Stephen spells colour without the 'u'.

"Oh?" Stephen asks, hoping to tread lightly, but inquisitive all the same.

Lucas takes a moment, knowing Stephen isn't going to snap as the silence fills the room, swoops around the pair, pulls them into itself.

"I just... can't relate. Sorry." Lucas admits, looking into Stephen's kind eyes finally.

"You don't have to relate."

"Oh." Lucas replies, small tears forming in the corners of his green eyes. "I guess... I just don't know what it's like... to be accepted..." his voice cracks, split apart by his creeping tears. "or even... to be loved... like that."

Lucas' words fall out of his mouth like a confession of guilt, thudding onto the floor, heavy and all encompassing, as salt streams from his eyes.

He's petrified, unprepared for this much vulnerability, even after these many months.

"You don't... feel loved... by your parents?" Stephen asks, his voice soft, like he's the safest place to land.

Lucas shakes his head ferociously. Thousands of memories flooding his brain. Years and years of raised voices, misplaced rage, and nights crying silently and holding onto a pillow for dear life.

And of course, there were good times, but they always came at a cost. A price Lucas often felt he truly couldn't pay.

Stephen squeezes Lucas' hand, unsure if going in for a hug is too much for this moment.

But he needs not wonder, for his question is immediately answered.

Lucas pulls Stephen into the tightest hug, fierce and frantic, clinging onto him for dear life.

Breathe in. Feel the heartbeat. He's here. Right here.

"I'm so sorry." Stephen comforts, rubbing Lucas' back.

"Me too."

Part 6

So, I Just Wanted
To Check In

Ste
Fri 24/08/18 19:22
hey!! it was really special to
learn more about you tonight
ty for sharing!

Lu <3
Fri 24/08/18 19:25
Thanks for listening
You're brilliant at it ♥

Ste
Fri 24/08/18 19:25
i'm really glad 😊
btw don't worry about telling people
idk why i brought that up 😵

Lu <3
Fri 24/08/18 19:26
What if we kept it on the table?
still need a little time
but I do want to 😇

Ste

Fri 24/08/18 19:26
😊!! but ur sure?

Lu <3
Fri 24/08/18 19:26
In a week or two I will be. Is that ok?

Ste
Fri 24/08/18 19:26
😊😊 absolutely 🖤

Lu <3
Fri 24/08/18 19:26
Thank you 🖤

Part 7

The Fruits Of Our Texts

"Morning you two!" Holly calls, entering the staff kitchen and noting the tension she's cutting into. "Something going on here? Everyone good?"

Stephen looking to Lucas, checking if it is ok to proceed.

Lucas giving a soft nod, a small smile, and taking a sip of his green tea.

"We've been, like, seeing each other, and we're gonna... sorta, like, start telling people." Stephen explains, bouncing on the balls of his feet with excitement, huge grin on his face.

"Fuck off." Holly responds, looking from one to the other, as she goes through the seven stages of grief in a few seconds. "I shit where I fucking stand. How did I not see that?!"

She steadies herself on the door frame, one hand on her hip, staring at the tiled floor of the kitchen. Her eyes glazing over, as she processes the information.

Stephen shows his silent concern to Lucas, who gives him a reassuring half-smile, knowing this is just how Australians can be.

"The... the Chrissie party? Of course! You never came to Rush after the Chrissie party! But wait..." Holly muses, putting two and two together. "You two have been hiding this for... eight! Eight months? What is it... a baby? Gives new meaning to 'fuck me dead, bury me pregnant'!"

Lucas laughs, and so does Holly, while Stephen stares bewildered, feeling the odd one out once again, with Brits and Aussies somehow able to speak a language he's never heard, despite growing up a scrappy Philly boy.

"You alright, New York?" Holly asks, between cackles. "you don't speak 'shit cunt'?"

"Leave him alone! He's a sweet cunt." Lucas retorts, laughing with Holly.

"Yanks don't have jokes, New York?" Holly asks, hanging onto the doorframe, doubling over.

"W-we have jokes, I just generally don't, like, use the c-word so much."

The response does nothing to quell the shared laughter between Stephen's ex and current lover.

It's interesting, the odd change that working for this stiff multi-national has had on him over the years. Too strait-laced now for harsh banter, and yet, still too working-class and queer to ever feel he could truly belong in these Old Money halls. But he's here now, so he might as well make the most of it.

Even if the most of it is being the butt of the joke.

"Don't make fun of Ste!" Lucas swoops in, well, seemingly. "He can't say 'cunt', or he'll have his contract terminated."

"They'll put him on the next fucking plane!" Holly jumps in.

The pair cackling so loud, their amusement ricocheting around the tiny kitchen, circling Stephen in a ridicule of his own making. At least he knows he has a type.

"I get it." Stephen deflates. "I'm not very proud of being American right now either."

"Oh no!" Holly covers her mouth, appalled behind her hand. "Fuck. I'm sorry. Too far?"

"I'm sorry too." Lucas pipes up, looking like a deer in the headlights.

"It's... how you say, like, 'no worries'." Stephen jokes, adding jazz hands, and a half-smile.

Holly looks from Stephen to Lucas, as Lucas looks from Stephen to Holly, a silent processing of Stephen's je ne sais quoi, and realising in real time why he's so appealing.

"You're... you're a total dork, aren't ya?" Holly accuses, smile apparent behind her hand.

"I know... isn't it sexy?" Lucas asks, looking Stephen up and down.

"I'm right here! You two are the worst!" Stephen faux-protests, hands on hips, tapping his foot.

"I'm sorry, New York." Holly jokes, bringing her hand down, and crossing both over her heart in put-on sincerity. "I should have *never* joked about how hot and dorky you are. And I also *never* should have said 'cunt', that was a real cunt move."

Holly's laughter fills the kitchen again, Lucas joining in, and Stephen soon following, barely believing the subject was supposed to be: 'Stephen And Lucas Are A Thing Now'.

Part 8

I Actually Love Emails!

From: Rhys Goncharov <rgonc@holmsyorke.com>
Sent: Monday, 10 September 2018 10:06 AM
To: Susan Leung <sleun@holmsyorke.com>
Cc: Lucas Watterson <lwatt@holmsyorke.com>; Stephen Herzig <sherz@holmsyorke.com>
Subject: FW: Disclosure Of Workplace Relationship

Morning Susan,

As discussed, I'm escalating this to you.

Please find attached the Disclosure Of Workplace Relationship form, concerning Stephen Herzig (Global Markets Junior Manager, ID 543-972) and Lucas Watterson (Commercial Banking Australia Manager, ID 397-182)

Please advise next steps at your earliest convenience.

Thank you,
Rhys Goncharov (they/them)
Employee Management, Human Resources
Holms & Yorke Bank Melbourne

Part 9

You, Me, And
Susan From HR

Susan enters her office, carrying a penguin mug, with a Rooibos tab hanging out the top in one hand, and her work phone in the other.

She pays no mind to the pair sitting in chairs facing her desk, as she walks in, slipping the work phone into the huge pocket in her oversize crème cardigan, and reaching up to tuck a stray lock behind her ear, running her hand along her French braid, checking it's keeping her long, dark hair in place.

Stephen and Lucas look up nervously, as she sits in her penguin-covered office chair, and jiggles her mouse.

"You'd think someone just fucking died." Susan jokes, her cultivated Australian accent broadening with her quip.

She laughs to herself, and takes a sip of tea

Lucas tries to let out a laugh too, but it comes out sounding like someone punched him in the gut, while someone else held his nose.

Stephen is just sitting there, silently, knees up and thighs tense. The brash Australian humour not tickling him once again.

"Alright, ok... no one's getting deported, so you two can knock this racket off." Susan gestures at the pair, bringing up something on her computer, and placing the mug down next to her numerous penguin knick-knacks.

A silent nod from Stephen, unnoticed by Susan, and a short 'yes, of course' from Lucas.

"Ok, so... you two have been in a romantic relationship for a few months now?" Susan asks, her accent returning to metropolitan as she looks over her bifocals at the pair.

"Well... um... I don't- would we call it a relationship, Stephen?" Lucas stammers, crunching himself up and pressing his arms into his middle.

"I, like... you know... I would, like... maybe say that..." Stephen attempts, looking from Lucas to Susan feverishly.

Susan sits back in her chair and pushes up the sleeves of her cardigan, resting her elbows on the chair's arms, and clasping her hands across her saffron dress shirt.

Raising an eyebrow, she looks over the two as though she can't believe the charade she's witnessing.

"Here's the thing: I'm just ticking boxes here." She states, matter-of-fact and professionally exasperated. "So, have you two been getting together in any way that isn't just friendly for a few months?"

"Um... we- um... yes, yes we have." Lucas affirms, unfurling slightly.

"Good. And... you're both aware that romantic relationships between co-workers are discouraged?" Susan asks, fiddling with her penguin-decorated lanyard.

Lucas opens his mouth to speak, before realising Susan is about to answer her own question.

"And discouraged doesn't mean... never allowed." Susan states, leaning forward, and focusing on her computer screen again. "And of course, we, as in HYB, don't want to be seen as discriminating against your relationship, due to its..." Susan looks over the pair again, and pointing back-and-forth. "Nature. That's our official position."

Lucas leans back, uncrumpling most of the way, arms still around his middle, mind running rampant, trying to process those words.

While Stephen relaxes his legs, and looks over to Lucas, hoping to catch a glimpse of what might be going on inside Lucas' head, to no avail.

"Does that mean, that if one of us wasn't a man, this would be different?" Stephen asks, baffled by that information, and unable to stop himself.

"Is one of you trans?" Susan asks, leaning forward and raising her eyebrows with the unmistakable concern of someone considering having to re-do paperwork. "Because that's a whole other thing, and we're not trying to hit discrimination bingo here."

"Oh, no... I'm not, like... like, we're not..." Stephen turns again to a still zoned-out Lucas, giving him a gentle nudge. "Are you? Like, nonbinary or something?"

"I don't... th-think so?" Lucas muses, woken from his haze. "How would I know? I th-think I'd probably... know, right?... or..."

"Look, I don't mean to be insensitive." Susan cuts in, taking off her bifocals, and placing them on her penguin-filled desk. "But listen, if you're both pretty sure you're cisgender men, I'm going to need to finish this meeting."

Susan leans back in her penguin chair, and watches the two, waiting for a confirmation, with a no-nonsense expression that could freeze hell over. That's HR for you.

"Yeah... a cis man." Stephen nods.

"Yeah, me too." Lucas agrees.

"Alright, so as I said, officially, we don't want to be seen as discriminating against a couple that is two men, right?" Susan asks, gesturing to check there's mutual understanding.

Stephen nods, Lucas following.

"But of course, unofficially, my opinion, off-the-record..." Susan continues, the pair tensing up, expecting some sort of abuse. "Is that I also don't care. But, don't do anything fucking stupid like screwing in the office."

Those final words cut through the air like throwing knives, Stephen catching Lucas' eye, communicating a shared silent panic.

Regardless, Susan gestures for the two of them to leave, leaning forward to type on her keyboard.

Stephen speaks some words of thanks, and Lucas echoes them, the pair trying to get out of her office as soon as possible.

Both hastily walking a fair way down the corridor, Stephen stopping in his tracks, before checking they're alone, and leaning into Lucas, close enough that only Lucas can hear.

"Do you think she knows?" Stephen whispers, looking up and down the corridor again, before continuing. "About us 'screwing' in the office?"

"I don't fucking... I mean, she might, but how? Are there cameras?" Lucas whispers back, panicked.

"No, there's not..." Stephen thinks, before realising. "The key cards."

"The fucking key cards. Shit!" Lucas vents, speaking in full voice, and covering his mouth as he realises.

Lucas checks the corridor again, no one to be seen, but it doesn't mean no one can hear. He uncovers his mouth, and motions that they should get walking.

"Look, it's obviously... like, maybe not completely ok... but, like sorta... ok *enough*, or we'd both be fired by now." Stephen asserts in hushed tones, as the pair hurry along the corridor together.

"Ste I'm not being funny but, I'm not really looking to get anywhere close to fired, this job is literally my ticket to stay here." Lucas replies, matching Stephen's hushed tones and hasty gate. "I have to stay here."

"Lu, it's my ticket too." Stephen whispers back. "In here."

Stephen stops in his tracks, opening the door to the fire escape, and holding the door for Lucas.

Lucas looks around one final time, and hurries into the concrete sanctuary.

"I fucking like it here in Melbourne, Lu. And... I really like you... I'm sorry, I got caught up."

Stephen's words bounce around the concrete walls, before bouncing into Lucas' head, catching him off-guard.

"You... *really* like me?"

Stephen can't hide his furrowing brows, Lucas Robin Watterson sure is an interesting experience.

"Yeah, I really, really like you, Lu." Stephen replies, his face softening, as he leans against the wall, watching Lucas with the same intrigue as when they first spoke at the Chrissy Party last year. "Why else do you think I, like... kept trying to get to know you?"

Lucas looks to his shoes, shuffling his oxfords in embarrassment. It doesn't matter who it is, it doesn't matter how much interest they show, there's still a huge part of him that can never believe it.

"Well, when you put it like that." Lucas shrugs, chuckling softly.

Stephen takes a few steps towards Lucas, running his fingers along the canary railing, ever the flirt.

"And..." Stephen begins, nearing Lucas, and catching those green eyes. "Here's the real part: I wanna keep getting to know you."

"Really?" Lucas breathes, almost inaudible in his smallness, ashamed to feel so needy.

"Of course." Stephen smiles, his eyes ever warm, his tone forever kind.

Lucas reaches his fingers out, running them along the railing as well.

Stephen noting it, inching closer, slowly, carefully.

The fingers meet, intertwining, silent and beautiful, small and true.

Lucas pulls Stephen into a hug, hands splaying out, reaching touches all over Stephen's shoulders, neck, back; just wanting, hoping, to feel as much of him as possible, to assure he's really here.

Stephen breathes into the embrace, eyes closing, hands reaching around the small of Lucas' back, simply caressing, no pushing or pulling, just present.

"I'm sorry I'm so bad at this." Lucas apologises, his chin resting on Stephen's temple. "You've been so patient, ever since the Christmas party. And I'm trying... but also... I don't want to go home, and I just... can't fuck this job up, y'know?"

"Yeah. I see you trying, like, and I hear what you're saying, like... about this job." Stephen soothes, meaning every word of it.

"And my contract's up for fucking renewal in, y'know, two months."

Lucas presses his fingertips into Stephen's back, pulling them closer, feeling his heartbeat against Stephen's, closing his eyes tight, breathing it all in.

"I forgot about that. Shit." Stephen laments.

"Me too. I got so excited about telling people." Lucas replies, edging closer to what he really wants to say. "And I'm not ready to go home."

Maybe he can say it. Maybe Stephen will hear him. It's right there on the tip of his tongue. He can do this.

"I don't think I ever want to go home."

"You don't have to." Stephen assures.

Part 10

Making The "Christmas" Party Interesting, And By Interesting, We Mean Queer

"Yeah, it's a bit dodgy, but what are ya gonna do?" Holly calls out over the music, craning her neck, showing the water banana on her shoulder. "I wanted a plant, and why not something Mauritian? Gotta represent, aye."

She shrugs, covering her brown skin, rebuttoning her violet shirt, and turning back to face the huddling group.

Stephen silently reviews the time he's spent with Holly, trying to piece together why he never knew about that tattoo, catching Uhai's eye, and immediately softening his expression, hoping he wasn't looking like a creep.

Tucking her shirt back in, and looking to Stephen, Holly points at him with her drink.

"Do you have any tattoos, New York?" Holly asks, taking a sip.

"Yeah... like, I have... like, a... pink triangle." Stephen stumbles, hastily taking a sip of his own drink, not looking anyone in the eye.

"Oh right." Lucas pipes up for the first time tonight, noticing no one else seems to understand the significance of Stephen's words. "I've been thinking of getting a cigarette." He adds, a small smile on his face, hoping his meaning and humour come through.

Lucas' words cause Stephen to look up, the two sharing a knowing look through the cluster, as the others around the circle continue the conversation.

Pointing to his drink, Lucas mouths 'refill'. Trying to provide enough cover for Stephen to have reasonable doubt.

Stephen silently nods, looking Lucas up and down, in a manner he'd never dared to before.

"We're gonna top up." Lucas explains to the group.

The others remain unphased, having moved on to Uhai's explanation of her white ink tattoos, which sat beautifully on her dark, Sudanese skin. She's regaling the circle with the story of her husband creating one of the designs as a wedding anniversary gift, as the others nod along, enthralled by the process, but the intrigue is missed on Lucas and Stephen, making their quiet exit.

The pair make their way to the drinks table, each hoping the other might broach the same question, sneaking looks at each other.

"So, you-"

"I, like-"

They share a nervous laugh.

"You first." Stephen offers.

"So, you... have that, um... tattoo for the reason I'm... um, assuming?" Lucas asks, pouring Solo into his work mug.

"I'm bi, yeah." Stephen answers. "You're not drinking?" He asks, noting Lucas wasn't adding spirits to his soft drink.

"Eight years sober this month." Lucas explains, tipping his mug slightly, before leaning in and stating: "And me too, by the way... the um, thing."

"Well, aren't you more interesting than you seem." Stephen muses, a devilish smile dancing on his face.

Stephen leans back slightly, really taking Lucas in for the first time, six months after this Lucas guy's move to the Melbourne office.

Lucas giving a little playful wiggle at the attention, smiling cheekily.

"Checking me out, are you Mr. Herzig?" Lucas flirts, placing his mug down and playfully running his fingers around the rim.

"Mr. Herzig?" Stephen asks, taking a step in, and leaning close enough to whisper in Lucas' ear. "Are you looking to call me 'Sir', Lucas?"

Lucas feels his heart race at those words, Stephen can read him like a book. And in the presence of their colleagues, at the office Christmas party, it's exhilarating. Perhaps, even, a move that could have dire consequences, just the kind of activity that gets one Lucas Robin Watterson absolutely losing all sense.

"Please tell me we can go somewhere else and at least..." Lucas asks, his eyes slamming shut, his body frozen in place, clutching this mug with his fingertips, waiting for instruction.

"At least, what, Lucas?" Stephen whispers, moving his hand along the table, and wrapping his fingers around the base of Lucas' mug, gentle and provocative.

"I... don't... um, I'd like to tell you what I like, Mr. Herzig, can... can um, I please t-tell you those things in private?" Lucas requests, head absolutely spinning by how fast this is moving, body aroused by that exact sensation.

"Follow me." Stephen instructs.

He swiftly walks out into the corridor, turning left, heading towards the toilets, Lucas hurrying behind him, not sure how this looks, or if anyone was even paying attention to the pair. The others huddling in small groups, or dancing around, engulfed in music, and bathing in cheap, colourful, party lights.

Stephen is several strides ahead of Lucas, seeming to disappear into the men's toilets, but when Lucas catches up a moment later, he sees Stephen holding the door for him, leaning one hand up towards the top of the door, and one on his hip, a smile painted on his gorgeous face.

"Hey." Stephen says, gesturing for Lucas to walk in first. "So, tell me... things."

He slinks in behind Lucas, pushing himself up, and sitting on the counter, in between one of the post-modern sinks, in the incredibly well-kept, black-and-grey room.

Lucas leans one hip against the sinks, crossing his feet and arms, closed and defensive, the sudden change from the dark, loud, crowded room, to this empty, bright one, seeping into his soul.

And he can see his own fucking reflection, never a good time.

"Um... I don't... now it feels a bit... exposed." Lucas says, shrugging and looking about himself suspiciously, as though someone else is hiding in here.

"Well, despite the long-standing tradition of queer men meeting in bathrooms," Stephen states, bouncing off the counter, "I'm happy to go wherever you can feel comfortable. Especially since..."

Stephen trails off, walking toward Lucas, running his fingers along the counter, then stopping a few paces from Lucas, and leaning in with a feminine flirtatious flourish, lifting his back leg up slightly.

"Especially since..." Stephen repeats, playful and disarming. "You're saying you have things you simply **have** to tell me."

Lucas can feel his heartbeat in his dry throat, as his pants give away just how exciting Stephen's teasing dominant side is.

It's seen by Stephen, who's eyes dart down to Lucas' arousal, and back up to his caught-out expression.

Stephen gives a little smile as he admires his handy work, before strutting to the door, holding it open for Lucas once more.

"Wherever you want to go, Watterson." Stephen prompts, his free hand on his waist, his posture malleable yet commanding.

"Mhmm..." Lucas tries to get out, still standing against the counter, completely enamoured by seeing this whole new side to Stephen.

Sure, he'd noticed the Yank was good-looking, with his thick curly hair, olive complexion, and strong features. He is hot stuff, and Lucas sees it.

But there's that other element of attraction, that isn't really about looks. How someone carries themself, how their voice changes when they flirt, that electricity of being alone with them, knowing you both feel it, the air pressure changing, the calm before the thunderstorm that rips through your body. Destructive and radiant.

And for Lucas, finally bearing witness to this extra, and all-important element, well, it's causing tingling in places which had been dormant for so long, they'd seemed to die off.

"Right... and, um... we, um... ok, this way." Lucas stumbles, shaking himself out of his own thoughts.

He makes his way to the door, takes in the sight of Stephen one more time, then heads out into the corridor, and in the opposite direction of the party.

"Your office?" Stephen teases, as he jogs a little to catch up to Lucas' nervously fast gate. "That's sorta... 'the boss and the secretary' of you."

Lucas can't get any words out, try as he might, it's just strained noises and the occasional 'um' or 'you see', as he continues to speed-walk to his office.

"I wasn't saying that's what I'm expecting, by the way." Stephen clarifies, not wanting to put any pressure on Lucas, and hoping his words come across as such. "I was just... teasing a bit. But I'll, like... shut the fuck up until- oh."

Lucas stops dead, still as stone, in front of his office door, one hand on the handle, turning to face Stephen, avoiding eye contact, as he prepares himself. The suddenness of it all causing Stephen to, indeed, shut the fuck up.

"I just... it's um... I'm not r-ready to do... um... anything." Lucas stammers, Midlands accent seeping in, nervous, shuffling his feet, continuing to avoid Stephen's eyeline. "I just, um... w-wanted some privacy to t-talk... is that ok?"

"Of course, Lucas." Stephen reassures, his tone warm and sincere. "I wasn't, like, expecting anything either, to be like, totally clear. Talking is good by me."

Lucas breathes a strained sigh of relief, a weight lifting from his shoulders.

"It's just, um..." Lucas begins, opening the door, and walking over to his desk, turning on the lamp. "It's been a w-while..." He turns to sit on the desk, while Stephen stays in the doorway. "Not just with a m-man, but, um... with anyone... so... um, t-talking is all I can do right now."

"Yeah, hey... I get that, like..." Stephen nods, Philly affectations warming his words, tentatively walking in, pausing to see if he should join Lucas on the desk. "I like talking."

Lucas noticing Stephen's hesitation, appreciating the gesture of holding back for a clear 'yes'.

Pushing through his own hard-wiring, he motions for an unsure Stephen to sit next to him.

Stephen makes his way to Lucas' desk, flirtatious strut unfound, as he walks across the small, murky room, sitting with his hands under his thighs and legs dangling down, while he watches Lucas with a scientist-and-subject-like curiosity.

Lucas, on the other hand, is tense, leaning forward, hands on his knees, making himself small, staring at the floor, head racing.

He is intriguing, this Lucas.

Transferred from the London office, initially on a three-month contract, so keeps to himself at first. And here Stephen is, glad to not be the only fish out of water.

Alas, it remained an absolute task to get much out of this Lucas character, even now his contract has been renewed for twelve months.

Holly and Stephen even made a game out of it.

If one can have a conversation with Lucas, for more than thirty seconds, the other one buys you a coffee the next morning. But neither of them could seem to win.

Once, Holly got to about twenty seconds, when she'd asked if he'd heard about the Frida Kahlo exhibit at the NGV International, and turns out he'd already gone. Which at the time didn't seem all that fitting, but now, it makes perfect sense.

A piece falling into place in the puzzle.

But finally, it seems the evasive Lucas is open to getting to know someone in the office. And one Stephen Alan Herzig is perfectly happy sitting, watching, waiting.

"So, you... um, you got me pr-pretty good, when you s-said, um..." Lucas begins, cutting through the silence of the dim room. "When you s-said... that I... like to... um, call people 'sir'... I mean, or 'ma'am', or, um... other th-things... I, um... I like th-that."

Stephen simply continues watching the awkward and tense Lucas, as he's speaking his words, eyes fixated on the carpet, Stephen responding with a quiet 'uh-huh'.

"And... um, I also d-don't really like much... um, how should I s-say this... m-much reciprocation... if you... get what I'm s-saying."

"I... definitely do, yeah." Stephen nods.

"And I... don't, um... d-don't often find people who are... um, into that... so I'd rather... w-wait until... I do." Lucas explains, becoming more and more tense as he elaborates. "If you follow what I'm s-saying."

Lucas gives a little shrug, but his shoulders stay up, adding to a tiring tension all over his body.

"I absolutely follow what you're saying, Lucas." Stephen reassures, maintaining his studying gaze and respectful distance. "And like... being dominant is something I can... really enjoy, like... with the right person."

The words wash over Lucas like a refreshing breeze on a scorching day. A small mercy in the dead centre of suffering.

A taut Lucas taking in a deep, painful breath, eyes vice-tight, rolling his head up, letting out a loaded sigh, and doubling over with relief.

"Thank fuck for that!" Lucas blurts, sitting up again, so much of that strained tension melting away. "I just... um, I never know how th-that's going to go... but, um... you s-seem to sort of... y'know, so..."

"Yeah, I'm a switch vers bi disaster, so, like..." Stephen teases, giving Lucas a little shoulder-to-shoulder nudge. "Don't worry about me not, like, knowing about kink stuff."

Lucas smiles to himself, and at last, looks to Stephen, waiting with a warm smile of his own.

"So, are you... like, one of those men who doesn't kiss other men?" Stephen asks, sensing his guess might be right, but hoping he's wrong.

Their short-lived shared glance ending, Lucas' eyes returning to the carpet, tensing all over immediately.

"I... I haven't."

"Oh..." Stephen replies, his tone carrying the hurt of a correct guess. "May I, like... ask why?"

"Um... I don't know... just, um... a mix of, um... w-working class Midlands shit and... um... general, um... s-sexuality things."

"Oh." Stephen responds, more understanding than hurting. "I'm sorry to... hear about that."

"Th-thanks." Lucas responds, glancing briefly to Stephen, putting on a half-smile, as Brits tend to do. "I th-thought maybe... um, my time in London w-would, um... dampen it... s-somewhat... but there's a lot of men... just like me in London."

"Right..." Stephen nods, hoping to coax more out of Lucas, gaze soft and watchful, tone gentle.

A pause. Perhaps Stephen's efforts are in vain. Perhaps that was all Lucas can share.

But alas! Too hasty by far! For the man speaks.

"Do you... kiss?" Lucas asks, tentatively, his green gaze flitting in Stephen's direction, but never meeting brown eyes. "Men, I mean."

"I, like... yes. Usually, yes."

Stephen's words dancing over to Lucas, hitting Lucas' ears, causing a wave of regret. Flashes of men's lips, shoulders, thighs, necks, hands, all unkissed. If only.

"Do you... want to..." Lucas tries, his eyes returning to the carpet, glued and focused, shoulders up, neck tense, his crossed ankles pressed so firmly, they might snap. "W-want to... k-kiss me?"

Of course, Lucas couldn't see, he wouldn't dare glance over, but Stephen's soft smile widens, as Lucas' words finally reach him, watching, waiting a beat for Lucas to look.

But he can't wait forever. So, whatever.

"Yes, absolutely." Stephen declares simply.

Tone kind, warm, without flirtation or tease, as though this was something outside of romance, and yet far more important, far more meaningful.

"Then..." Lucas begins, body still tight enough to break at any moment, but face finally turning, eyes laced with a boundless longing, a man lost at sea for so long. "Can you... pl-please?"

Stephen nods simply, inching his hand along the desk, reaching Lucas' fingers, white-knuckling into the wood.

Slowly, carefully, as though one wrong move would tear something deep inside Lucas, Stephen traces his fingers over Lucas' fierce grip, an electricity sparking from his very fingertips, as he's finally feeling Lucas under his touch.

A tingle radiates from Lucas' strained hand, more than simply the physical tension releasing, also the sheer sensation of gentle touch, wary, youthful, boyish, yet caring.

Stephen is telling Lucas that despite his joyful anticipation, he'll pull back at any moment, for any reason.

New. Small. Exciting.

Lucas slowly relaxes his hand under Stephen's, fighting against a million voices swarming his head, attempting to communicate that he wants this to continue, somehow, in any way, please.

Stephen tucks his fingers under Lucas' palm, squeezing gently, wanting to feel more of Lucas, if only, maybe, Lucas'll have him.

Lucas feels his shoulders coming back down, his neck relaxing, his crossed ankles unfurling, his body feeling more welcome here than he ever has anywhere.

He watches Stephen, unsure if his body is saying enough, or if he should speak louder. Deciding to do his best impression of a nonverbal shout, he leans forward, heart racing, eyes fluttering, breath heaving.

Stephen hearing Lucas loud and clear, bringing his other hand up to Lucas' cheek, running his index finger over Lucas' earlobe, receiving a small whimper in return.

He smiles, watching Lucas for a lingering moment, wanting to pull this moment like taffy, stretch it out, savour it.

He guides Lucas close, into blessed space, inviting intimacy, serenity, rescue.

Their lips meet, soft and cautious, swimming with longing, communicating a sadness, a cutting off of the self, a muting of the supposedly unseemly, all in an attempt to reach the summit sooner.

Deeper, more passionate, tongues on tongues, and yet it's not sex, it's not desire, it's a deep wound being tended, the shards of salt being picked out one by one, precise yet messy, care in the middle of battle.

It floods Lucas, lighting him up, opening doors he'd closed long ago, wonderful and healing, stinging like an exposed nerve.

It too much, it's not enough.

Lucas pulls back.

Stephen watches. He felt it. He heard exactly what Lucas told him in that kiss.

A hand still on a cheek, faces still so close, neither moving.

"Are you... ok?" Stephen asks, gently bringing his hand down from Lucas' cheek.

Lucas doesn't know. He can't know. Feeling too old to be this young, to be this new, and all the while, so deeply embarrassed that he's never done this before.

"Yeah." Lucas lies, pulling his hand out from under Stephen's, clutching his middle with both arms. "M-maybe we sh-should go back to the... um, the p-party... pick this up... um, another t-time."

Stephen nods, taking in a defeated breath. The mystery of Lucas will have to wait for another day.

And hey, the kiss was nice, so it wasn't a complete swing-and-a-miss.

Standing up slowly, as though sudden movement would spook Lucas, he speaks into the small, dark room.

"Of course, yeah." Stephen replies, as he smiles at a retreated Lucas. "I'll head back now, and, like... see you there... sorta, whenever."

Lucas silently nods at Stephen's words, once again watching that ever-so-intriguing carpet, his mind running rampant.

Stephen pauses for a moment, unsure if he should try a touch of the arm, or even just wait for a verbal reply, but decides to leave without any further words or actions.

He turns and quietly opens the door, one last look back, Lucas remaining still and holding himself, and he leaves the man to this thoughts, closing the door with a soft click, not wanting any sudden noises right now.

Part 11

I'm Actually So Chill In This Hallway Right Now

He stands in the silence of the well-lit corridor, questioning if this is a path worth following, or if he'll even get a chance to follow it, perhaps Lucas will pretend he doesn't exist after the break.

Despite it all, there was something about Lucas, something Stephen had to know more about, an all-consuming zeal born from a craving he knew all too well, like he was meeting a version of himself from his high school days, before coming out, filled with a fear of how it might all go.

And for Stephen, those fears were unfounded, but maybe there's something to be known here, the enticing and intriguing mystery of the unknowable, and yet somehow familiar. Perhaps decoding this fearful, closed-off, unsure man, who is so much of who he once was, is going to teach Stephen about himself.

Or perhaps he can give Lucas what he wished he had back then.

Bonus points: he is a fellow non-Australian.

It is an interesting kind of loneliness for Stephen, being here in Melbourne. It's not simply being away from his family and community. There's community here too, even in the fabled halls of Old Money WASP Big Business, Holms & Yorke Bank.

No, there is something else. Little cultural touchstones that he was always discovering, and small conversational confusions or missteps, all leaving him feeling like a fish trying to walk on land.

An odd otherness that seems foolish to complain about. Especially with the state of The Land Of The Free And The Home Of The Brave in this, the year of our Lord, twenty-seventeen.

Lucas is same-same, but different. It's refreshing, comforting.

And despite the exchanges being short, there has been alleviating moments of 'isn't this some Twilight Zone shit?' between the two of them.

Such a subtle joy, in being able to jokingly lament with one another, about compulsory voting, or supermarket duopolies, or the mining industry, for only one reason: it's different to home.

That difference, bringing with it a curious mix of intrigue and alienation. Like being in an empty airport, a sense that somehow, this is less real, but knowing that simply can't be true.

And maybe Lucas can't be real either, maybe that's why Stephen's so fascinated.

Regardless of why or what or who, he's hooked, and he's going to enjoy the thrill.

Stephen leans against the wall, taking it all in for a moment, the taste of Solo on Lucas' tongue, that tang of lemon, the sweetness of sugar, and there was something else filling his senses; vibrant, cleansing, distinctly Australian, perhaps eucalyptus, but he couldn't be sure.

Another piece of the mystery to add to the bulletin board.

Part 12

No One Can Know

Dark. Frozen. Alone.

The faint sound of the party slowly flowing under the door, momentarily tuned out by the moment, by Stephen. But now, alone in his office, the background comes into focus.

Lucas has never tasted another man's lips, but he also hadn't tasted alcohol in eight years.

He wants more. Of both. Of either. Anything. Just another taste.

But no. That's not for him. A taste leads to a sip. A sip leads to downing the whole thing. Downing leads to some weed, some pills, some coke.

Something. Anything. More and more and even more.

Until there's none of him left, until he's lost hours and days and doesn't know how he ended up on this stranger's floor, or what he did while there.

Or maybe he doesn't want to remember.

He can't have anything.

Nothing he likes, nothing he wants, nothing at all.

No, no, absolutely not.

It has to be taken from him, dangled in front of him, just out of reach, and still he's told no.

Because he knows, he knows all too well how deep the spiral goes, that at rock bottom he'll grab a shovel and dig his own grave, that if the shovel breaks, he'll get down on his hands and knees, and scrape and drag and burrow, until his hands are bleeding, and his fingernails are split and cracked, and the dirt is seeping, deeper and deeper into his very being, until he's crying and screaming into the abyss, hoping if he only digs far enough, he'll fall right in, and be lost in the ether so deep, he'll never be found.

For no one can ever see him falling, let alone when he finally becomes one with the deep, dark, empty. They'd never understand.

For without understanding, there can be no sympathy, and that has to be true, or Lucas wouldn't have spent the past thirty-seven years punishing himself any chance he got, and trying to escape his own punishment at every other chance.

It just has to be true. It absolutely has to.

For here he sits.

Knowing that if he moves, he'll chase Stephen, he'll go get a drink, he'll say something, do something, that he can't take back. He'll be lost to himself, he'll be scared of himself, of his hunger, of his anger, of his deep, searing hatred.

He doesn't like that person, he doesn't want to be that person, not again, not here, not now.

He has to stay, he has to wait, he has to breathe, eyes closed, arms wrapped around his middle, body tense, fingers balled in fists, hoping, biding his time, easing, pushing, pulling.

Soon, soon, very soon.

Just a little bit longer, just a little bit more, just a-

Fuck it.

Lucas pulls a hand up. Fist tight. Ready.

Face grimacing. Fast breath in. Punch down. Hard.

Thigh throbs. Fist stings. Breath out.

Fist up. Breath in. Punch down.

Muscle aches. Breath out. Face scrunches.

Another. And another. More. And more.

An elbow around the mouth. A muffled scream. A red face.

A burning thigh. A stinging fist.

Elbow down. Staring ahead. A man alone.

A distant party he's no part of.

Part 13

I Love Texting

Someone I Hardly Know!

Stephen From Work
Fri 22/12/17 13:52
hey!! how's your time off 👀
must be nice to not have a hangover?

Lucas W
Fri 22/12/17 14:01
Yeah no hangover for me 😇
Good time
You? Any plans for the break?

Stephen From Work
Fri 22/12/17 14:06
no plans!!
already had my little summer hanukkah 😎
nothing else planned 😟

Lucas W
Fri 22/12/17 14:08
Too bad 😟 Im not doing
christmas coz its just me
not enough time off to go all the way home

Stephen From Work

Fri 22/12/17 14:09
yeah same for me!! such a long flight
ur welcome over btw 😊
not just for holidays lmao

Lucas W
Fri 22/12/17 14:09
Haha. Thanks. No thanks for now tho
Need some rest after this big year lol

Stephen From Work
Fri 22/12/17 14:10
i hear that lmao open
invitation if you change ur mind!!
happy holidays 😊

Lucas W
Fri 22/12/17 14:10
U too. I know im late but chag sameach 😄

Stephen From Work
Fri 22/12/17 14:10
aww ty!! invite open all break 😊

Lucas W
Fri 22/12/17 14:11
Thanks 😇

Part 14

I'm Perfectly Casual And Chill

And Not Desperately Trying To

Get In Touch And Hangout And

Get To Know You At All! Genuinely,

I Don't Even Care Either Way!!

I Hope That Helps!!!

Stephen From Work
Wed 27/12/17 13:16
hey!! how's your break 👀

Lucas W
Wed 27/12/17 13:37
Hi! Yeah pretty alright haha
getting plenty of sleep 🛏 You?

Stephen From Work
Wed 27/12/17 13:42
yeah same 😊
i went to the beach!! you been?

Lucas W
Wed 27/12/17 13:43
I haven't haha was it nice?

Stephen From Work
Wed 27/12/17 13:43
the best!! maybe we could go together lmao

Lucas W
Wed 27/12/17 13:47
Sounds nice I have to politely decline
haha burn like nobodys business 😌

Stephen From Work
Wed 27/12/17 13:47
oh too bad lmao if you change ur mind
invite's open 😊

Lucas W
Wed 27/12/17 13:49
Thanks! It's nice to be included haha
sorry I can't make it this time 😇

Stephen From Work
Wed 27/12/17 13:49
i'm very happy to include you 😊
enjoy ur week and happy new years!!

Lucas W
Wed 27/12/17 13:49
You're so nice haha
thanks happy new years 🎊

Stephen From Work
Wed 27/12/17 13:49
😊

Part 15

If I Never See Another "haha" Again, It'll Be Too Soon

Stephen From Work
Mon 01/01/18 12:06
get up to anything last night 👀

> **Lucas W**
> *Mon 01/01/18 12:21*
> Not really watched the fireworks on
> telly and went to bed 😇 You?

Stephen From Work
Mon 01/01/18 12:25
i went to hollys house party!!
thought i might see you there lmao
she said she invited you 😊

> **Lucas W**
> *Mon 01/01/18 12:26*
> Yeah she did haha.
> I'm just relaxing this break
> no parties for me 😇

> **Lucas W**
> *Mon 01/01/18 12:26*
> How was it tho?
> A good time?

Stephen From Work
Mon 01/01/18 12:27
yeah for sure!! pretty low key 😊

Stephen From Work
Mon 01/01/18 12:27
but nice to see everyone!!
and meet some new people lmao

Lucas W
Mon 01/01/18 12:27
Sounds fun. See you wednesday 😇

Stephen From Work
Mon 01/01/18 12:27
ok. see you wed 😊

Part 16

You Seemed
Super-Not-Into-Me,
And What's Like,
Up With That?
Asking For A Friend Actually!

"Hey! Lucas!" Stephen calls, jogging a little to catch up with Lucas after the nine-thirty. "How was your break?"

"Yeah, good." Lucas curtly replies, staring ahead as he doesn't make any attempt to slow down.

There's a pause. A collective holding-of-breath. And a shared inability to read the situation.

"Hey, listen..." Stephen tries again, his breathing becoming uneven as he tries to keep up with Lucas' anxiety-charged power-walking. "Should I... like, back off?"

Lucas stops.

It takes Stephen a moment to respond. Doubling back and huddling to one side of the corridor with Lucas.

Others walk by them, nodding, half-smiling. Background noise and ticking timebombs incarnate.

These Others might notice. They could clock this strained exchange. Or maybe not.

Stephen and Lucas are motionless, waiting for the corridor to clear.

The Others thin out, chatter clearing, echoes fading.

Until finally, it's only Stephen and Lucas.

Lucas deflating, his entire body curling in on itself. He looks up to Stephen, a feat in and of itself, as Lucas ordinarily has half-a-head on Stephen.

But here and now, he's small, hoping to hide away within himself. And through thick dark eyebrows, his green gaze shoots from the floor, to Stephen, then stays low.

Stephen watches Lucas. Who is this man? And why does Stephen want to figure him out so desperately?

He watches Lucas, an overlapping web of exposed nerves, ready to recoil at the slightest sign of resistance.

And all Stephen can think of is taking Lucas in his arms, his fingers splaying out in Lucas' salt-and-pepper hair, his chin resting on Lucas' forehead, as Lucas buries a head into his suit. But he can't do that. Not here and now.

"So, um…" Stephen begins, looking around quickly, and stepping in just a little. Not close enough for suspicion, but enough for privacy. "Do you want me to… back off?"

"No."

It is small, in length and volume. Tiny in the stretching corridor. Not daring to bounce around and be heard by anyone else's ears. Only for Stephen.

"No?" Stephen clarifies.

"No."

Stephen nods in response, unsure if Lucas can see him.

"Ok." Stephen replies, his voice quiet, as though Lucas unlocked the secret code for Whisper Mode. "It's just that... like, when I was trying to... over the break-"

"No one can know." Lucas whispers, interrupting with the incredible power of quietness. "At least for now."

Stephen soaks in Lucas' rushed and tiny words, as though he's hearing language for the first time, trying to decipher meaning, unsure if there is any to be found.

"Ok." Stephen manages.

"And... what if someone... someone *from work* would have seen us." Lucas whispers, raising his head for a moment, catching a glimpse of Stephen's caring, yet deciphering, eyes. "Seen us... together."

It slots into place in a moment. The paranoia. The hiding. The list of go-to excuses. Stephen knows it well. Even if it feels a lifetime ago for him.

"Right."

"And I… y'know… y-you." Lucas continues, hushed as ever. "I do. B-but… it's just… I c-can't do… d-dating or anything… but I do… y'know…"

"You like me?" Stephen asks, smiling bashfully.

Lucas nods. As small as his words, but heard by Stephen.

"I like you too." Stephen replies, boyish and giddy.

Lucas looks up, not just glancing, but his whole being moving up and up.

Just brave enough.

As though in the nick of time, Stephen has grabbed his arm, as he was slipping from a cliff's edge, and now Stephen's pulling him up to the solid ground. Straining, dragging, pushing. Until finally. He stands on the rock, unsteady but planted.

He looks at Stephen, a tether to this world. But he can't tell Stephen what this means to him. He isn't allowed those words.

So, Lucas simply looks, standing tall again, eyes meeting eyes, observing, absorbing, enjoying. Looking from Stephen's giddy smile, to the now prominent freckles under his olive skin, highlighted by his recent time in the sun. Up to the faint crow's feet in the corners of his dark eyes, and down to the smile lines framing his sincere giddiness.

He is joy, he is light, he is Stephen Alan Herzig, and Lucas wants to be just like him.

But nothing is that easy.

Part 17

blink-182 (album) Track 12, 0:49

"New York!" Holly calls, bounding into the kitchen, reusable mug at the ready. "Excited to be back at it?"

Stephen half-smiles, nodding insincerely, unable to match Holly's plentiful energy.

"That's the enthusiasm I love to see!" She jokes, pointing to an awkward Stephen. "Plans for the weekend?"

Stephen wordlessly shrugs.

"Wow, talkative this arvo, aren't ya?" Holly teases, rummaging in the fridge for her lunch. "Something wrong?"

A silent shake of the head.

"Alright." She concludes, placing her lunch in the microwave.

Holly removes the lid to her mug, bringing it to her lips, blowing on the steam, looking to Stephen, and raising an eyebrow, tilting her head, a roguish smile on her face.

"Well... if you're up for it..." She flirts, stepping closer to Stephen. "I was gonna head to Rush on Friday. Have a think, open invite. Got some coke. Could be like the old days."

She steps back, considering him for a moment, before being interrupted by the beeps of the microwave, and leaping into action.

As a wordless Stephen stands, blank and barely responsive, she grabs her hot lunch, and mug, heading for the corridor.

"Yeah, I'll... think about it." Stephen finally pipes up, half-smiling once more, unseen by Holly.

She raises a hand in response, not looking back, turning and disappearing, her footsteps fading.

It's just Stephen. In his now all so familiar dichotomy of loneliness and company.

Memories of past Fridays at Rush flashing in his mind's eye, a kaleidoscope of colours, tableaux of bodies, that beautiful feeling of queerness and nightlife.

Holly's body against his, the taste of coke right in the back of his throat, The Veronicas soaking into his bones, bassline rumbling under his feet.

Kissing Holly deep and slow, tasting the vodka on her tongue, his fingers dancing over that dip in the small of her back, her hands gripping his arse.

People talking outside the toilet cubicle, her thighs around his face, as he kneels on the cold tile floor, as she grabs his hair with one hand and stifles her moans with the other.

Dreamy. Electric. Heavenly. Another world accessible with a door fee.

Part 18

Go, Go, Go!

Lucassss
Fri 12/01/18 17:16
Coast is clear 😇

Stephen From Work
Fri 12/01/18 17:19
packing up now
got caught up talking to uhai 😊

Lucassss
Fri 12/01/18 17:19
Ok. ready and waiting

Stephen From Work
Fri 12/01/18 17:20
omw 👀

Part 19

I Actually LOVE Words!

~~(And Having Sex With Men)~~

"So, should we start with safe words? Do you like the traffic-light-system?" Stephen asks, taking off his suit jacket and setting it down on the couch. "Sorta... green, yellow, red?"

Stephen's been in Lucas' office many times, he knows the charcoal sofa, the black-out blinds, the walnut desk, that warm desk lamp. Oh yes, it's familiar, but of course, it's not.

Perhaps he was too ambitious to have been thinking of this since the office party, but he has been. And what? He's a man with an active imagination. Is that a crime all of a sudden?

There's truly no repression like British repression, and he's about to experience the eager testament.

Lucas contemplating Stephen's words of traffic lights, as he sits seiza-style in the space between his desk and back wall, ready to go.

"I, um... I j-just want you to... um... r-ram it down my th-throat..." Lucas replies, looking up at Stephen. "like it's a... a, um... g-glory hole thing, b-but... y-you can see me... so..."

"But what if I'm doing something that you... don't like and you want me to, like, stop?" Stephen tries to clarify, pulling off his tie and unbuttoning his shirt. "That's what safe words are... for."

"Oh... um... it will be a little hard... t-to talk... um..." Lucas tries, words just out of his reach.

Having such a frank discussion isn't something Lucas anticipated, or encountered before. It's awkward, uncomfortable.

Somewhere inside, he knows this is wonderful, this speaks volumes about how Stephen sees him, cares about his comfort, boundaries, wellbeing.

But so much of him is fighting to just be here, to even share this small part of himself with another man. He isn't ready for the moving of mountains that is talking about what they're here to do.

Stephen unbuttons his cuffs, rolling his shirt up to his elbows, taking a moment to register Lucas' silence.

He looks over, spotting Lucas kneeling behind his own desk, and feels something shift inside him.

What a spectacle. The slightly older, slightly taller, and definitively more fidgety, Lucas Watterson. Ready and waiting. Already kneeling. As though it's the only place in the world he feels at ease.

Lucas feels Stephen's eyes on him, hoping he looks good, or sexy, or whatever he's supposed to look like, waiting to get a cock in his mouth.

Then, Stephen changes. He pushes his rolled sleeves up ever so, and he's smiling. Mischievously, playfully, brimming with absolute delight, bubbling just under the surface.

Stephen rests both hands on the front of his belt, tucking a thumb in slowly, moving rhythmically toward Lucas, floating across the office, an air of the sublime about him, with a smoothness, like a dancer, purposeful but controlled, and oh so captivating. His hips swaying and gliding, drawing in Lucas' keen gaze.

Mind filling, knowing what's behind that belt, and what's between those hips. Losing himself in the wanting, the anticipation, the sudden shift in the air, Lucas is completely present, yet exquisitely gone.

It's everything he missed, a liminal space in the body, a quiet in the soul, finally.

Stephen pauses at the desk corner, reaching out a finger, tracing a line, following his slow, enchanting steps, carefully, with intention, edging closer a waiting Lucas, watching all the while. Eyes never leaving eyes.

Stopping as he stands squarely in front of Lucas, barely any space between them, leaning against Lucas's desk. He glances down at his tracing finger, eyes indicating for Lucas will follow.

And Lucas does, of course. Under the spell of the divine.

Stephen traces his touch back towards himself, Lucas watching his fingers with bated breath.

The movement is light, gentle, serving to enamour, not dominate, not yet.

He draws his touch in, carefully, purposefully, reaching his hip, then splaying out his fingers, and feeling his way up his own chest, to his pecs, his neck, eyes closing, dancing his touch up to his cheek, over his earlobe, and along his jaw.

Lucas watches in absolute awe, it's like nothing he's ever seen. No masculine bravado pretence, but not wholly feminine either. As though Stephen actually knows how he likes to be touched, what feels good to him, as though his desire isn't something manufactured by media and social expectations, but curated entirely by Stephen alone.

Sure, he is teasing Lucas, but it's not a performance, it's an invited display, a come-hither by demonstration, and a sneak peak of what Lucas is missing out on.

"If you like..." Stephen speaks into the heavy silence, his words breathy, and his tone teasing. "I can just do it myself... since you won't give me a way to communicate with you."

Lucas stares up, speechless, cheeks red. He's been absolutely got.

"How about, if anything is too much, I'll squeeze you behind the knee?" Lucas blurts out, wanting and rushed.

"Yeah, I mean, bottom's choice." Stephen remarks, caressing his chest, fingers circling, short nails running against the cotton of his celadon button-up shirt. "And what about words? What would like me to say... or not say... to you?"

Lucas looks up at Stephen, his mouth watering with the hope of what is about to happen, and his mind fogging at sight of Stephen's self-touch.

"Lucas?" Stephen calls, playfully, his hypnotising caressing continuing. "I don't want to say anything you wouldn't like."

"Um… I don't know…" Lucas confesses, looking wide-eyed up at Stephen.

"Well… what words have you… enjoyed in the past?" Stephen asks, halting his self-teasing, and bobbing down to Lucas's level.

Their faces close, Stephen gently bringing his middle finger up to trace along Lucas' bottom lip.

It's electric. It's intimate.

Lucas' lips are tingling, his breathing ragged. This is completely new. And it's all because of Stephen.

"Um, just, loads of words…" Lucas lies, head flashing with some choice flashbacks of less-than-enjoyable encounters that never scratched that itch. "Bitch, slut, cocksucker, whatever."

Stephen smiles, silently noticing Lucas' reactions to his touch, to his approach, as though this is untrodden ground for Lucas. What an incredible high, to watch someone new, feel something new.

"Ok." Stephen speaks, still tracing his finger slowly over Lucas's lip. "I can maybe work some of that in, and what about praise?"

Only silence from Lucas, enthralled and lost.

Stephen tries again.

"Someone... might like to be told how good they are... at sucking dick." Stephen suggests, delighting in Lucas becoming putty in his hands. "Or... maybe be reminded that they're... not allowed to cum, because they're so... good for me. Does any of that sound-?"

"I like the second bit." Lucas blurts, emboldened by desire. "But also, something like the first bit is good too."

"So, if I..." Stephen flirts, bringing his thumb up, to rest on Lucas' plump bottom lip. "If I told you how much I'd love to see those lips wrapped around my dick, would you like that?"

Lucas silently nods, his mouth opening at Stephen's words.

"And if I..." Stephen continues, moving his thumb just inside Lucas' lips, feeling the warmth, the softness. "If I said... I can't wait to see what a skilled cocksucker you are, would you-?"

Lucas cut Stephen off by taking his thumb into his mouth, running his tongue along the underside, causing a surprised 'ok!' from Stephen.

"You're eager, aren't you?" Stephen teases, raising an eyebrow.

"Mhmm." Lucas answers, circling his tongue around Stephen's thumb.

Impressed and aroused, Stephen's cock twitches in his dress pants, wishing it was a thumb.

"Someone's a good little slut, isn't he?" Stephen praises, pulling his hand back, eliciting a whimper from Lucas. "But are you ready to show me what you can really do?"

Lucas' eyes widen as Stephen stands up, and he feels the dynamic be created in a simple gesture.

A man standing over him, as he kneels before that man, keenly awaiting the chance to please. It's spiritual, heavenly, worship.

Stephen rests his hands on his belt, a smile crossing his lips as he sees Lucas' eyes fixating on those hands.

"Please, Mr. Herzig, I need it." Lucas pleads.

"What do you need, Watterson?" Stephen asks, undoing his buckle, savouring Lucas' watchful gaze.

"I-I... n-need your cock, Sir." Lucas pleads, looking licentious eyes up to Stephen's brown ones, hoping he looks needy enough.

"Where?" Stephen asks, grasping the buckle end of his belt.

In one ferocious movement, he whips the belt off with a hard tug, the end snaking around to slap Lucas across the face.

Stephen is still for a split-second, caught out by his own mistake.

Lucas closes his eyes, moans escaping his cherry blossom lips.

"Th-thank you, Sir."

"You like to be slapped?" Stephen enquires, undoing his top button, relieved his mistake was oddly kismet.

"Y-yes please…" Lucas begs, eyes fluttering open. "But pl-please… I need your cock in m-my mouth, Sir."

Stephen reaches down, cradling Lucas' face in his hands, Lucas keening into the touch, hot and depraved.

"Mmmm… please…" Lucas moans, his hands reaching up.

Stephen smacks those hands back down, eliciting a tantalising whimper from Lucas.

"Just for that." Stephen firmly states, unzipping his trousers tooth by tooth. "You have to be… on the balls of your feet to blow me… I want to watch you… work for it."

Lucas lets out a soft moan.

The prospect of working hard to give pleasure had never occurred to him, but it adds to his beloved feeling of being used, exploited, doing all the work for no reward. It's unfair, it's agony, it's like no drug he's ever experienced, and he wants to mainline it.

"Yes, Sir." Lucas agrees, moving to squat instead, resting precariously on the balls of his feet, as he grabs onto Stephen's thighs for balance, and dear life. "I w-want to be g-good for you."

"Then show me." Stephen commands.

Stephen hooks his thumbs into the waistband of his briefs, pulling down, revealing his hard cock, as it sits barely an inch from Lucas' lips.

Without a second thought, Lucas takes Stephen's entire length into his mouth, feeling the head hit the back of his throat, looking up to see Stephen's reaction. Hoping and praying his skills are satisfactory.

Stephen's tries to steady himself, his hips keening as the blessed bliss floods his system. He reaches down to grab Lucas' shoulder, his mouth falling open, as he takes in a sharp breath, and he tries to stay upright.

"Ah, Fuck!" Stephen calls out, his grip squeezing into Lucas' shoulder. "Y-you're fucking g-good at that, Watterson."

Lucas lets out a whimper, and feels his untouched cock twitch at the praise, the hum of his response resonating through Stephen, as Lucas continues to push that cock as far down his throat as possible.

"Uh-huh fuck..." Stephen praises, relishing in the vibrations. "D-do that again, bitch."

Lucas does as he's told, the feeling of being used and dominated rushing his system, lighting up his senses, electrifying his very being. He fervently hums another moan against Stephen's hard cock, as he slams it deep down his throat.

Stephen lets out a low, guttural moan, those vibrations sending tingles up his spine, as he enjoys Lucas' warm, slick, mouth eagerly devouring him.

It isn't quite enough for Lucas though; he needs to feel Stephen take sex from him. So, he releases his grip, not easy in his perilous position, and takes Stephen's hand from his shoulder, moving it on the back of his head, trying to signal he craves more force.

"A bit... rougher, Watterson?" Stephen teases.

Knowing full-well that's what Lucas wants, Stephen decides to make him really work for it, beg for it, be absolutely drenched in need before being granted it, and begins softly circling his fingertips in Lucas' salt-and-paper hair, while Lucas continues deepthroating like his life depends on it.

With no response, he is left with only one option.

He grabs a tuff of that hair, and holds Lucas firm as he pulls that head back, taking in the absolute vision that is Lucas.

Cheeks rosy, lips plump, eyes dazed. Craving, wanting, brimming with heavenly desire.

He bobs down, Lucas's grip failing him, hanging only by Stephen's grasp, firm on those locks.

Stephen rubs his nose against Lucas', a cute respite from domination, ensuring he has Lucas' full attention now.

"I asked you a question, Watterson." Stephen taunts, forehead to forehead, towering, cock hanging. "Do you... want it a bit more rough?"

"Y-yes, S-Sir." Lucas breathes, powerless and alive.

"How rough, slut?" Stephen asks, cock twitching at his own words. "I need specifics."

"I-I w-want you to fuck my..." Lucas blurts, his attention moving from Stephen's watchful eyes to that hanging, hard cock, causing his head to fog, and his heart to race. "my m-mouth like you f-forgot it's a m-mouth... like I'm a th-thing, n-not a person."

"Are you sure, Watterson?" Stephen asks, pressing his temple to Lucas' forehead.

"Y-yes, Sir…. very sure." Lucas pleads, eyes completely on that cock, hanging just out of reach. "I w-want you to pull m-my hair… use m-me… force my th-throat onto your cock… pl-please."

"Hmm… how about this?"

Stephen's words are barely out of his mouth, when in one quick movement, he straightens up, and tightens his grip on Lucas' hair, pushing that mouth onto his cock. Hard.

The sensation washing over his system with powerful force. Rolling his head back in delight.

And, just as swiftly, pulling Lucas all the way off. His cockhead resting on those plump lips.

"You like that?"

"Y-yes, Sir. Th-thank you." Lucas breathes, hands flying to Stephen's hips, tongue extending, trying to reach for Stephen's cock. "Just l-like that."

"Oh?" Stephen teases, sucking air in through his teeth, as Lucas' tongue is busy licking at his underside. "Just face-fuck you like the little bitch you are, until I cum down your throat?"

Lucas can only let out a delicious moan, brain completely fogged.

Stephen smiles knavishly down at Lucas, taking in the superb sight that is a vulnerable and wanting Lucas looking up at him, lost in the moment, loving every second of this.

He holds firm his grip on Lucas' hair, and pushes himself back inside Lucas' lips, a low groan leaving him as he feels his sensitive tip hit the back of that throat. Hallowed glory.

He relishes in the feeling for a moment, then begins moving, just as Lucas asked, watching those wide green eyes looking up at him with every thrust.

With his thighs burning, struggling to stay balanced, fingers gripping tightly into Stephen's thighs for support, his own cock screaming for attention. It is perfection to Lucas.

There's nowhere else he'd rather be.

"Take my dick, slut." Stephen moans, using Lucas, ascending to a higher plane, lost in elation. "You love that, don't you?"

Lucas vibrates a moan against that cock, as he watches Stephen's gratification. Controlled, red-hot, dazed. He can't get enough.

"You love being used... don't you, bitch?" Stephen growls, soaking in the sacred dominance, inching closer. "Just a hot mouth... for me to cum into."

Moan. Muffled by cock. Eyes fixed on the man above him. Watching the pleasure he's denied. Transcendent torment.

"You're gonna be... so good for me..." He breathes, pleasure building, mounting, layering, closer still. "And I'm not even... gonna touch you."

Another moan. Fingers digging into thighs. More. Just a little more.

"F-fuck... yeah, Watterson... I-I'm almost th-"

Strained whimper. An eager mouth pushing as vigorously as it's being pulled. Hard. Fast. Forceful. Just a bit more.

They both know. Almost.

A low, guttural, moan from Stephen, head rolling back. Ecstasy flowing through him. Pushing all the way down. Lifting, falling, euphoria.

Cock twitching. Once, again, another, and another. Hot cum spilling down a thirsty throat.

Alight green eyes looking up, watching another experience the orgasm he gave, vicarious, torturous, religious.

Stephen slides Lucas back, flinching at the aftershocks, as his spent, slick, cock escapes rosy cheeks and lewd lips.

Loosening his grip on Lucas' hair, those thighs giving out, falling forward, Stephen catching the exhausted form, forearms cradling underarms.

"Whoa, are you alright?" Stephen asks, gently guiding Lucas onto his backside.

"How... h-how was it, Sir?" Lucas asks in response, plopping down, ungraceful and weary.

"It... it was... wow." Stephen answers, steadying Lucas.

Lucas smiles to himself, faint and content, still completely engulfed in sex and control.

"Th-thank you, Sir." Lucas breathes, quiet and lost.

"You were so good for me." Stephen praises, gleaning Lucas hasn't left the sanctuary of kink just yet. "Such a good little slut for me."

Lucas looks up to Stephen, devotion and adoration in his green eyes, smile fluttering on his plump, soaked lips.

"I'm gonna get dressed and leave." Stephen states, bringing his hands up to cradle Lucas' face. "And only when I'm gone... you are allowed to jerk yourself off, like the desperate little bitch you are... Understand?"

Lucas nods, floaty and malleable.

Stephen smiles, bringing Lucas in slowly, their lips meeting, hot and wet, tongues tasting tongues, breathing each other in, passionate and messy, gentle and vigorous.

Head spinning as Stephen kisses him deep and loving, present in the bliss, and struck by the reality that he could've had this before. If only the stars had aligned sooner, and he'd been fortunate enough to meet someone like this.

Lucas kisses back, he's ablaze, starving, desperate, just a little more, a tad more could fix him, solve his every ailment, if only he could taste just a bit more.

Stephen feels it again, that hunger, that wanting, that palpable devotion, as though Lucas has never felt this free, this safe, this present. It's glorious and heartbreaking. And oh, is it moreish.

More and more, like teenagers here for the first time, taking it all in, like they'll never get another chance to kiss, to taste, to feel.

Stephen traces fingers up Lucas' torso, feeling the heat, the desire, the hunger, grabbing Lucas by the tie, pulling him closer, a moan reverberating through the kiss, Lucas lost in another act of dominance.

Delectable, sinful, otherworldly.

An oasis in the desert, Lucas has to stay as long as possible, he has to take everything he's given, it has to sustain him for who knows how long.

Stephen pulls back a little, Lucas trying to follow, unsatiated, still starving, absolutely on fire, Stephen holding himself over Lucas, watching him, taking him in.

Lucas looking up famished, none of his need diminished, wanting as ever, need sitting deep in his bones.

Continuing to try as he might, he lifts his head, hoping to touch lips to lips, Stephen pulling back playfully each time, holding Lucas firm by the tie.

It would be hilarious if it wasn't so painful.

Stephen mercifully leans back down, bringing the tie closer, laying a final, sweet kiss on Lucas' lips, eyes closing, a moment stretching.

He pushes that tie back, standing, pulling his underwear and trousers up, stowing his cock, and looking back at Lucas with a deviant wink.

Lucas remains frozen on the floor of his own office. Hands planted as though they've been tied down, body unmoving, as though if he's still enough, he'll be granted exalted temptation.

Stephen walks back to where he left his suit jacket, and fiddles with his sleeves, before sliding his arms in, and fixing the lapels, all the while sensing Lucas' eyes on him, and relishing the feeling.

Once he's dressed, he struts back to Lucas, squatting down, tracing a hand over Lucas' flushed cheeks, and along those plump lips, as Lucas looks up at him with those vivacious green eyes.

"Like I said... you can jerk yourself off... after I go."

And with those words, Stephen stands, grabs his backpack, and walks out of this office, leaving an exhilarated Lucas laying on the carpet.

Part 20

What If We, Like...
Talked To Each Other?

"It's just, I feel kind of mean not returning the favour, even in a kink context, it doesn't feel, like... talked out or something, if I'm making sense, like, I know-"

"Yeah, it's nice of you to be concerned." Lucas interrupts, unbuckling Stephen's pants, on his kneels behind his own desk. "But, it's the way I like it, and I'm enthusiastically consenting, ok? You're not coercing me or anything."

Stephen looks down at Lucas, it was only the fourth of their now weekly visits, but it was already feeling one-sided and hollow.

He is no stranger to queer men having specific hang ups and requests. But here, with Lucas, there is a feeling, something floating between the two, uncatchable and indeterminate, that has been crying out to him, if he could just get Lucas to open up, there could be so much more to know, to hear, to learn, under that reluctance to engage in mutual play.

Unaware that Stephen isn't present and ready to indulge in transgression, Lucas pulls down Stephen's underwear, and quickly realises he won't be able to deepthroat that cock from the jump.

Unphased, and keen to get started, Lucas licks and sucks the head, while pumping the shaft, barely even thinking of the person attached.

"I... I want to stop, please." Stephen pipes up, pulling away from Lucas' attempts to get him hard. "I... like... can we sit?"

Stephen dons his underwear and trousers, before walking across the dark office, and plonking down on Lucas' charcoal sofa.

He tenses up, closing off his whole body. Hands clasping and pressing between knees, feet crossing, head bowing. His body protecting him, as his mind and mouth seek to be brave.

Lucas reaches his shaking hands up to steady himself, standing cautiously, as he grips onto his walnut desk ferociously, his pale skin becoming white, as the desk serves to keep space between he and Stephen. Another instance of maintaining a barrier to other men.

"Can you... please join me, Lu?" Stephen requests, relinquishing one hand from his vice-like knee-grip, and patting the sofa next to him.

It's an odd feeling to be given a nickname. Strangely intimate, yet casual and chummy.

Lucas looks down at his white knuckles, and retracts them, fast and shameful, as his old defensive habits insist on dying hard.

Hugging his middle, Lucas smiles to himself, the simple gesture of a nickname, washing comfort over him, enough to join Stephen on the sofa. Not as Lucas, but as Lu.

The pair sit. The ease chipping away, as several quiet moments pass, and the two are encased in loaded silence, the hands of stillness pushing down upon them. Stephen trying to find his words, Lucas not having his in the first place.

It's youthful. Awkward. Desire held hostage behind the unknown.

Black-out blinds, closed and covering, intended to provide privacy for sin, now serving to keep out the intrusive evening Summer sun, threatening to creep in, and shed light where it's not wanted.

For another light is being shed inside.

The reality of simply being two people that don't really know each other, seeping painfully into their bones. Something so fundamental, skipped over, as one wished to jump into the ocean, never learning to swim.

"Ok so, yes, this *has* been really fun." Stephen speaks, continuing to look at the floor, hands gesturing in front of him. "But I feel a bit weird just, like… having you blow me and leaving, with so little kind of… talked about."

"But I'm into it." Lucas replies, the nuance unnoticed by him.

"Well, I'm not!" Stephen shoots out, his fanned-out hands freezing for a beat, before he realises his tone, pulling is hands back into a self-hug, before continuing. "I'm sorry, I didn't- I… ok. Even with the framework of like, kink context, this is still feeling very, like, one-sided for me… without, like, some…

talking. It's not just the action, but also, like, the why behind the action. Am I making sense?"

Lucas nervously nods, soaked in the shame of not truly considering Stephen's side, too preoccupied with his own mix of desires and inhibitions.

"Lu, I am attracted to you, and I would like to know enough about you to be sure that, like, even if this is just sex, that the sex is like, not just consented to, but also like… fully informed, on both sides."

Lucas lets out a small sound of agreement, feeling far more perceived by a man than ever before, despite their shared elusive gaze.

The silence returns, harrowing and uncomfortable. Speaking volumes.

Stephen sinks forward in his seat, hanging his head in his hands.

"Can you please say something?" He mumbles behind his palms.

"I guess… I… I don't know what to say."

Lucas' words are tiny, he's completely unequipped for this. Stephen speaks of things he's never even imagined.

"You could tell me if there's a reason for it." Stephen raises his head from his hands. "Like, is it an orgasm denial thing? Or like-"

"Yeah, it's um, the orgasm denial." Lucas lies. "It's just, um… h-hornier if the other m- um, person is in c-control, um… classic British repression."

Stephen looks over Lucas, gleaning those words aren't the truth, or at least, the whole truth. But this isn't his 'A Few Good Men' moment, he's not one to yell across a court room, and not only because he doesn't worship at the shrine of the American Freedom Machine; but also, because he's all too aware that many queer folks are moving at their own pace, fighting their own internal biases, and hoping, amongst it all, for a sliver of respite, a taste of connection, to soothe the wound of being The Other.

A fate whispered about, tales recounted with spite, in the broad daylight of the burning Summers, and in the dark corners of the freezing Winters, parents, teachers, and community, all telling of the horror that shall befall them, should they, in fact, turn out to be The Other.

And sometimes, even the smallest push is too far for those who aren't ready to face their own fate.

But maybe Stephen can cut his smallest push in half.

"Yeah." Stephen half-smiles, chin resting on his hands. "I'm a switch so I get it. Like, I guess I just... wasn't sure if there might be some... like, sexuality stuff to it, and I wanted to, sorta, offer some support in that... area. *If* that was the case."

Stephen's words wash over Lucas, as he catches the underlying meaning, feeling tears will their escape, and pushing them down in turn. Overcome with relief that if he was able to, he could possibly speak with Stephen about something he barely dared think of, even alone.

"Th-that's nice of you to offer." Lucas replies, voice cracking from those almost-tears, as he coughs, hoping to hide it. "But it's... um, y'know, not... it's n-not like that."

"Yeah... yeah."

Stephen's reply sits in the air, he heaves a heavy sigh, conflicted by a desire to know more of Lucas, and a want to meet Lucas where he is now.

He watches Lucas only for a moment, as Lucas fiddles and shifts, then looks to the floor not wishing to examine more than the man wishes to reveal. And chooses instead to allow the silence to once again fill the air.

There's an odd awkward comfort.

A feeling this tension can't end here and now, neither can simply leave, and there's certainly no sex on the cards. Simply a wordless agreement to absorb this moment.

Minutes pass. The inescapable sun still peeking around the black-out blinds. These Summer evenings, feeling more like afternoons. Two men sitting on a couch, more like scared kids.

"Maybe I should go." Stephen finally speaks into the dark, warm office.

"Oh." Lucas replies, knowing this was likely news. "Can we try again next Friday?"

"Yeah."

Stephen stands. Wanting, hoping, to pull Lucas into a tight hug, feel that body against his.

Instead, he takes the few steps to Lucas, and places a hand on his shoulder, Lucas looking up in response.

Eyes meeting. Quiet. Real.

Stephen nods. Lucas nods. Stephen leaves.

The bustling February CBD waiting for him.

The small room missing him.

Part 21

Oh, That's Me!

Stephen flops down onto his bed, squaring up to his reflection in the mirrored doors of the wardrobe.

There he is. Hot pink towel around his shoulders. White briefs. A light dampness from the shower. Just some guy.

Sun streaming in like daggers, ricocheting around like bullets, lighting up everything he'd rather not see right now.

Sullen eyes, puffy from tears, olive skin red from sobbing. He knows there's no shame in crying, but sometimes it'd be nice to not be faced with the aftermath.

It's eight o'clock on a fucking Friday night, he should be doing coke and going down on someone in a nightclub, like a proper queer. Not contemplating an early night, after some conversation with a man in a dark room, like he's in some period drama.

He's intrigued by Lucas, so sue him.

Barely two months since their office party kiss, and he's hankering for another bump.

The intensity in that man's eyes, as he looks up at Stephen, his flushed face after he gets a load down his throat, the way he absolutely drips desire and sex, as though he'll never be satisfied, as though he'll always be yearning, wanting, hoping.

Stephen eyes wander to his briefs, noticing arousal reflected back to him.

In a swift motion, he reaches for the towel around his shoulders, and pulls, whipping it into the clothes basket across the room.

Gently, intentionally, he draws the light, delicious touch of his own hand up to his chest, dragging the back of his nails up his neck, slowly, enjoying the scratches being left in his supple, damp skin.

He sees the wet spot forming from the decadent sensation, as he nears his jaw, and runs his touch up one side, reaching his curls, and splaying his hands out, his pinkie dancing along the back of his ear, his thumb tracing along the nape of neck, the rest of his fingers exploring those curls, massaging his scalp, relishing in the simple delight of touch, and the glory of watching his every move in the mirror.

Roughly, he grabs onto a tuff, and pulls hard, moaning into the empty room, cock twitching at the spectacle.

He looks at himself. Eyes lit up, filled with lust, cheeks blushing under his dark freckles, head tilted, a handful of his own hair.

He traces his other hand down from his shoulder, splaying fingers out across his chest, circling a nipple, watching himself, tightening that grip on his curls, and running a nail over that nipple, taking in a sharp breath at the exquisite feeling.

With watchful, licentious eyes, he drags those nails down his chest, across and over the pink triangle sitting on his ribs, leaving salacious marks as he does, hoping they'll stay until morning, a gorgeous reminder of how well he knows what makes him absolutely ravenous.

Nails reach the waistband of those white briefs, and he stands, sauntering closer to his reflection, wanting to watch himself more completely. Not simply sitting on the bed, but standing before himself, he's his own sub, and his own dom.

He looks over himself, hand in his hair, marks down his torso, skin hot, lips parted, ablaze with need. Eyes settling on his own cock.

'Take those off. Slowly.'

His internal voice commands. Dominant. Simple. Clear.

Releasing the grip on his curls, he drags his other hand down his chest, digging the nails in harder, following the scratches, a path to pleasure, paved by himself, now highlighted, bolder than before.

A thumb into the waistband, then the other, both running along the sensitive skin, nails marking as they go, slowly, with intention, and resting on the hips. Breath sharp. Eyes watching. Skin marked.

'Now pull them down. Good boy.'

Stephen does as he tells himself, inching down the briefs, purposefully, teasingly, little by little, looking over himself with absolute eros, as the band reaches his cock.

Watching enraptured as he reveals the base to himself, sliding the band along his length, bit by bit, tantalisingly, really making himself want it.

Taking in a sharp breath as the band reaches the head, inching over the sensitive tip, and finally, his cock emerging from the white cotton.

'Now all the way down. Quickly.'

In one quick motion, he flings the briefs down his legs, the fabric settling at his feet.

'Keep them there, bitch. Feet planted, ok?'

Nodding to himself, he takes in his naked body. Nail marks from his neck, down his chest, through the triangle on his torso, along his hips, his olive skin flushed all over, cock hard and waiting.

He is the Sir and the slut. And he's nowhere near done with himself.

'You can touch anywhere but your cock. Until I say.'

A moan escapes his lips. One of his absolute favourites.

He runs horny hands up his thighs, splayed and wanting, touching all the skin they can, grabbing, massaging, exploring.

Knees keening slightly in response, whimpers falling from his lips, hands wandering up and up.

Fingers travelling in, around, under, tracing the sensitive spot deep between those thighs, pressing circles into the skin, massaging, watching his cock twitch, untouched.

'That's it... Keep going... Such a good, obedient slut for me...'

Circling harder and harder, trying to hit that good spot from the outside, the friction becoming painful, just as likes it.

His other hand squeezing nails into his thigh, skin sinking, sting rushing up and down his legs, moans cascading from apricot lips.

'You like the pain, don't you?'

"Yes..."

One hand pulls up. Slaps down. Hard. Arse stinging.

'...you like being teased...'

"Mmmm... yeah..."

Circling stops. Other hand still. Skin freezing hot.

'...and you like being told "no"?'

"I do..."

Both hands off. Eyes studying. Chest heaving.

'Well fuck you, I won't give you a "no"...'

"You won't?"

Hands travelling up thighs. Slow. Burning.

'I'll give you thirty instead... I'll count you down...'

Stephen nods.

'...thirty...twenty-nine...'

Spit on his hand. Gripping his cock. Pumping furiously.

'...twenty-eight...twenty-seven...'

Other hand cupping his balls. Squeezing. Releasing. Repeating.

'...twenty-six...twenty-five...'

Hips bucking. Knees keening. Heels lifting.

'...twenty-four...twenty-three...twenty-two...'

Breath hitching. Moans escaping. Cheeks blushing.

'...twenty-one...twenty...nineteen...'

Pleasure building. Mind fogging. Tingles running rampant.

'...eighteen...seventeen...sixteen...'

Strokes feverish. Urgent. Ignited.

'...fifteen...fourteen...thirteen...'

Moans growing. Louder. Bouncing.

'...twelve...eleven...'

Tension building. Edge approaching. Body red.

'...ten...'

"Please, please, please..."

Squeezing tighter. Pain rushing. Whimper.

'...nine...'

Eyes fluttering. Lip between teeth. Neck tensing.

'...eight...'

It's right there. Almost. Nearly.

'...seven...'

Thrill flooding, moans lewd, rhapsody.

Ecstasy rushing the spine, flooding the mind, vision blurring, euphoria tearing back down.

Moans carom around, like the evening February sun, saturating the bedroom in the enchanted essence of Summer sex.

Stephen floats back, cock drained, balls aching, cum on the mirror.

He heaves through his aftershocks, tracing a thumb over the slick cockhead, gentle, calming, grounding.

Breath steadying, teeth releasing lip, vision coming into focus.

Stephen looks over himself, satisfied, glistening, in need of another shower.

He brings his slick hand up to his mouth, tongue out, ready. Fingers in, tasting himself, tongue circling, lips pursing.

A drop falling from his mouth, dripping down his chest, and over the abrasions, as he sucks the cum from his fingers.

Lewd. Wanton. He could go again right away.

Part 22

You Good?

Stephen From Work
Fri 02/02/2018 20:56
hey!! how are you?
sorta an intense talk today ☺

Lucassss
Fri 02/02/2018 21:01
Hi. Yeah I'm fine 👍
Happy to keep plan for
same time next week. U?

Stephen From Work
Fri 02/02/2018 21:02
yeah totally next fri, ur office
enjoy ur weekend 😎

Lucassss
Fri 02/02/2018 21:02
Cool 😇 Enjoy ur weekend too

Part 23

Some Good Fucking News

From: Susan Leung <sleun@holmsyorke.com>
Sent: Monday, 8 November 2018 10:22 AM
To: Lucas Watterson <lwatt@holmsyorke.com>
Subject: FW: Melbourne Contract LW 397-182

Morning Lucas,

Please find attached details of your renewed contract.

Any questions, let me know.

Cheers,

Susan Leung (she/her)
Human Resource Senior Manager
Holms & Yorke Bank Melbourne

Part 24

Twelve! More! Months!

"I'm just so glad!" Lucas gleams, placing the takeaway on his kitchen island. "Ste, I'm genuinely so fucking chuffed."

Stephen bounds in after him, filling the minimalist, drab, all-white, kitchen with his gracious, glowing being. Face radiant, eyes happy, absolute light.

"It looks good on you." Stephen affirms, placing a flirtatious hand on Lucas' waist.

"On me? You're one to talk." Lucas muses, moving closer to Stephen. Guided, seductive.

Lucas beams down at Stephen, reaching a hand up to cup Stephen's face, running a thumb along the cheek, those freckles faded, as this winter stretches and sticks like honey, keeping Stephen from getting his beach time well into November.

"You're really so beautiful." Lucas states, like it's obvious, like anyone would see Stephen as he sees Stephen. "How do you do that, genuinely?"

"Be so beautiful?" Stephen smiles, his gentle fingertips tracing shapes on Lucas' back. Absentminded, loving, easy. "I mean, like... having good company helps."

Stephen watches Lucas, looking up into his green eyes, full of the compounding ease of hours, weeks, months, spent sweating, touching, kissing, and discussing, holding, learning. That undemanding bliss of knowing another.

And yet, still there is more to see, to understand, to know, for there remains flecks of uncertainty, excitement, newness, sewn into the tapestry of affection and connection.

"And… I'm gonna be sincere and American about this for-"

"As long as you fuck me after, I'll allow it." Lucas interrupts, a devious smirk dancing on his plump lips.

"Oh, do I *have* to fuck you?" Stephen retorts, twinkling eyes laced with faux annoyance. "I was going to, like, just eat this phở and leave."

"Fuck you." Lucas volleys, smile turning positively devilish.

"As I was saying…" Stephen returns, pulling Lucas closer, intimate and comfortable. "I'm going to be sincere and American, so you'll just have to deal with it."

Lucas pretends to consider Stephen for a moment, an air of false deliberation, barely covering the cheekiness underneath.

"I'll allow it."

"So good of you." Stephen replies, going from sarcasm to sincerity in a moment. "Ok, the thing is… now we can spend, like, the Summer break together, and sorta… like, if you like…" Stephen sheepishly looks away for a moment, as though what he's about to say is too intimate for comfort. "We could both, like… take time off next year, for… like, Passover… and sorta, like… go somewhere, like, when it's not as busy…"

Lucas holds back a smile, unseen by Stephen, as those brown eyes continue to look elsewhere, waiting for something clear and verbal.

But without that something, Stephen rushes to continue.

"…and I don't mean Passover like, we'd 'do' Passover, like… I'm talking about that time of year, and like, whatever, I just mean… it's a nice excuse to take time off and see some of this country and-"

"Do I just say, 'yes' and 'yes'?" Lucas smiles, with deep, affectionate, joy. "Is that what I say?"

"Is that… what you wanna say?" Stephen bashfully asks.

"Absolutely!" Lucas asserts, placing both hands around Stephen's face, cradling. Meaningful and pure. "Yes, and yes, Stephen. Of fucking course."

"Cool." Stephen says simply, dripping with unused nervous energy.

"Ok then, cool." Lucas muses, looking into Stephen's eyes, breathing him in, the apprehension, the love, the joy, everything.

"No Jew shit for you though." Stephen jokes, complete with lively grin and playful shrug. "I'll be Jewish on my own, by myself."

Lucas feigns offense, moving his hands to his own face, mouth agape, and stepping back from Stephen's embrace.

"Oh, gatekeeping your religion, history, *and* culture from me?" Lucas jokes, voice high-pitched and melodramatic. "What kind of boyfriend are you?"

"Ok, first of all: I should have never taught you the word 'gatekeeping' and second of all: boyfriend?" Stephen smiles, looking Lucas up and down.

"Are we not... boyfriends?" Lucas asks, charade dropping in an instant, becoming bashful and quietly eager. "Can I... can I be your boyfriend?"

Stephen leans back against the kitchen island, gaze up at the ceiling, beaming, specks of disbelief and relief in his smile.

"Yes please!" He agrees, turning to Lucas, joy shining through. "Yes please. I would very much indeed like to be your boyfriend, and for you to be my boyfriend."

"That's me." Lucas glows, stepping into Stephen, hand on the island, hips close. "Ok. I'm your boyfriend."

"My boyfriend who..." Stephen returns, hand over island hand, lips leaning into lips. "Doesn't do Jew shit with me."

"I mean..." Lucas volleys, smirking as lips brush lips. "I wasn't attracted to the rituals."

"Oh, so now you *don't* wanna do Jew shit, wow." Stephen jokes, leaning back, putting on offense, hand clutching invisible pearls. "The antisemitism really jumped out. I see how it is."

"My rouse! No!" Lucas quips, hands to his forehead in false defeat.

"Yeah, once you got that boyfriend status, antisemitism, to my face." Stephen jests, looking about himself in soap-opera theatrics. "I'm shocked, I'm appalled."

"Well, we had a good run." Lucas banters, pointing as though he's headed for the door to his own apartment.

"Yep. So, I guess you better take my phở and head out." Stephen nods, gesturing from Lucas to the takeaway with faux-expectation.

"You're not gonna fuck me?" Lucas whines with fakes disappointment.

"I don't know..." Stephen pretends to muse, pulling Lucas into him, hands fanning out on Lucas' lower back. "I'm pretty sure I still feel... fetishised by your... goy eyes-"

Stephen's words are broken by a loud cackle, radiating from deep in his stomach, along both their chests, and out into Lucas' kitchen.

"My goy eyes?!" Lucas laughs stumbling back, catching himself on the island. "What is that?"

"Your lustful goy eyes!" Stephen repeats, between echoing cackles. "You're looking at me with your lustful goy eyes!"

"Goy eyes? Isn't that... isn't that..." Lucas volleys, barely getting the words out between strained breaths and ear-splitting cackles. "That's the... the guy who painted... painted 'Saturn Devouring His Son'?"

"That's the guy!"

"Francisco Goy-eyes!" Lucas volleys, both hands steadying him against the island now.

The laughs bouncing around the room, a chorus of joy, connection, a shared language surrounding the two. Exquisite and effortless.

Stephen steadies his heaving breath, dabbing his watering eyes, and letting an 'alright'.

"Lu, I'm being serious, when I say this." Stephen flirts, looking Lucas up and down, as Lucas catches his own breath. "I value you as a person, I enjoy our bits and our laughs, I really do, but..."

"When are we gonna fuck?" Lucas finishes Stephen's sentence, as he notes salacious eyes on him.

"Took the words right out of my mouth." Stephen flirts, closing the space between them once again.

"And usually you're doing that." Lucas replies, far too much sass in his smile. "But the words are your cock."

"Do I do that a lot?" Stephen asks, genuine concern lacing his words. "Are you sick of it?"

"I could never be." Lucas shrugs, that sass hanging around. "It's great banter. Gets me every time."

"Are you fucking joking?" Stephen asks, face alight with mischief. "Are you fucking joking about me pulling my cock out of your mouth while we were secretly fucking in your actual work office, where we make millions of dollars for rich people?"

"Oh, so I can't say anything anymore?" Lucas faux-protests, dramatic hand on his forehead. "You're silencing me? A white, British man? Oh no, how will I ever feel important again?"

"Maybe after we decide if I'm gonna bend you over before or after we eat this pho." Stephen retorts, grinning fiendishly.

"So, you *are* silencing me?" Lucas continues, banter taking precedence.

"I'm doing the opposite actually." Stephen answers, sarcasm running through his words. "I'm asking you a question, because I just have to know what you think, as a white British man. Like, I'm *totally* dying to know."

"I think… that I'm gonna be in the bathroom for fifteen minutes, and when I come back…" Lucas replies, leaning in, caressing noses. "I would very much humbly request that you put your cock in my arse, slap me, and choke me. Is that ok, or am I being silenced again?"

"Yeah, you'll be silenced… when I put my hand around your throat." Stephen retorts, laying a soft kiss on Lucas' lips. "Now go clean your ass."

"Fuck you." Lucas jokes, lips grazing lips.

"Fuck you." Stephen volleys, before taking half a step back.

Brown eyes boring into green, playful tongues waiting behind fiery lips, chests rising and falling in anticipation. A touch of space between them.

Stephen grabs Lucas's tie, pulling hard, mouths falling into each other. Lips parting, tongues meeting, finally. Firm and intense.

Stephen kisses him with command. You're mine. Right here. In this moment. You belong to me. Feel my desire. Drink in my fire.

Lucas melts under his dominant wanting, twisting, bending to his whim. Closer, more, never enough. You can do anything, I am yours, as the world fades away, it is just us here. Sex, lust, surrender.

Stephen pushes Lucas back, holding the tie firm. Rough and clear. He wants Lucas aroused, hoping, waiting.

"Clocks ticking. Be a good boy."

The words cutting through, hitting Lucas' ears like delicious sin, Stephen's tone completely transforming, opening that place within Lucas. A key in a lock.

Stephen releases Lucas' tie, dancing his touch down Lucas' torso, feeling the heat, Lucas is here, yet gone.

Part 25

I Guess You Could Say
I'm A Romantic
I Do Like To Get
Dicked Down At Home
So... I Guess That Counts!

An eager Lucas bounces out of the bathroom, Stephen plops his phone down, and springs across the apartment.

"Can I use a washcloth?" He asks, dancing a thumb under Lucas' chin. "I wanna freshen up."

"Oh... that's very... polite."

"Only the best for my..." Stephen teases, placing both hands on Lucas' flushed cheeks, jiggling Lucas' face. "boooyyyyfrieeeeend."

"Fuck off. They're under the sink." Lucas retorts, scurrying from Stephen's grasp and heading to the bedroom. "I'll get everything set up in here."

"What if we... fucked on the couch?" Stephen suggests, turning on his heel to face Lucas.

He turns back, perking up at the idea. They have been pretty domestic, location-wise, so on the couch? Why not!

"I'll get set up on the coffee table then." Lucas agrees.

"That's a good boy." Stephen praises, bouncing over to slap Lucas' arse.

Lucas smiling in response, his cheeks blushing.

Stephen disappears into the bathroom, Lucas busying himself grabbing lube, condoms, and tissues from the bottom drawer in his bedside chest, and bringing it into the living room, setting it all down on the coffee table.

Then he's just sitting, waiting. Noticing the dampness in his seat.

A moment later. Click of the bathroom door. The beautiful face of one Stephen Herzig. Like colour rushing a black and white scene.

Lucas watches eagerly, glued in place, hands on knees, sitting forward, as Stephen saunters over, an all-too-familiar look on his face.

He reaches a corner of the muted yellow couch, running a finger along the textured material, stitch by tantalising stitch, closer and closer, while Lucas remains watching, dripping with need.

The finger reaches Lucas, tracing down the cushion, and over to his thigh, Stephen's hot breath on his neck, as the finger draws up his hip, over his torso, across his chest, hand splaying out, covering the neck.

He pushes down. Hard. Sudden. Lucas rocking back. Head hanging over couch cushion. Looking up at him.

Body ablaze, with a hand around his throat, Lucas watches Stephen, brain fogging, wanting, hoping.

Stephen squeezes. Counting one, two, three, four. Releasing on five.

Lucas gasping, eyes fluttering, skin tingling.

He leans down. Leaving a kiss on Lucas' forehead. The heat radiating up. He wants another taste.

In one swift move, Stephen jumps over the couch, landing on top of Lucas, straddling thighs, taking Lucas' face in his hands, guiding them into a kiss.

Lips tingle, rushing the system, tasting arousal.

Grinding down on Lucas, relishing in feeling Lucas excited and ready, rubbing his own hard cock between them, covering Lucas completely, commanding and ablaze.

Feeling taken, surrounded, Lucas kisses back as thanks, begging and hoping for more, everything, anything, deeper, slower, faster.

Both hands move to Lucas' nape. Into his short hair. Grabbing firmly. Pulling hard.

Lucas hanging in the ether, lips plump, gasping, alight with desire.

Stephen lifting his hips, clothed cock flush with Lucas' throat, grinding.

Watching in a daze, Lucas feels the firmness on his skin, his breath rushing along Stephen's cock, the friction causing a twitch from Stephen.

He rubs and thrusts, Lucas looking up in absolute devotion, hand in hair, cock against throat.

"Stay still, bitch." Stephen commands, releasing his grip from salt-and-pepper locks.

Lucas does as he's told, watching Stephen trace fingers up his own thighs, and button by button, opening his shirt, grinding steady and controlled all the while.

Eyes locked on Lucas, releasing buttons, moving up his chest, reaching his tie, and tantalisingly, with intention, pulling it down, slow and disciplined, then, in one swift toss, throwing it across the apartment.

Smirking down at Lucas, he pauses at the top of his thrust, pressing his hard, clothed cock firm against Lucas' throat, as he brings one hand up to his own open collar, and traces the touch down, slowly, gently, with seductive malice.

Lucas looking up with reverence, mesmerised.

Oh, how he'd give Stephen the moon and the stars if he could. But his body will have to suffice.

Stephen grabs a fistful of the fabric, his other hand joining, and quickly, forcefully, throws the shirt off, and out into the space, gone from this realm.

"P-please..." Lucas whispers, voice straining against hips, wanton eyes looking over Stephen's body.

Stephen promptly pushes back, standing over Lucas, shirtless, hands by his sides, hips forward.

"Get it out, bitch." Stephen commands, voice low and dominant.

Lucas complies, his own cock twitching as his fingers hurriedly unbuckle Stephen's belt, unzipping trousers, and pulling down briefs. He pauses, looking up to Stephen, awaiting further instruction.

Stephen reaches down, grabbing Lucas by the tie, drawing him closer, resolute and potent.

Hands flying to hips, tongue extending, lips meeting cock.

A deep moan falls from Stephen's lips, as Lucas teases, savouring.

"Good boy, just the tip." Stephen praises, watching Lucas' lewd licks.

He traces his grip to the knot of Lucas' tie, slipping fingers under, pulling the collar out.

"Shirt off. Now."

Lucas complies, fingers flying to buttons, skilful mouth never pausing, relishing in complete submission. Shirt discarded. Eyes focused on Stephen. Resolute.

Suddenly, Stephen pulls back, Lucas trying to follow, hoping to taste more.

Stephen reaches for his belt, hooking a finger in the buckle, and pulling it off in one fast swoop, tossing it next to a waiting Lucas. He dances his fingers along the length of his hard cock, Lucas's lustful eyes focusing on his every move, as he circles his thumb over the tip, then sinks his fingers into the waistband of his briefs, and buries his cock under the fabric.

Lucas' eyes flash concern, looking up to Stephen, silently asking if this is over.

The response is Stephen kneeling before a sitting Lucas, an unfamiliar sight, Lucas frozen in confusion and arousal.

Stephen unhooks Lucas' buckle, pulling the belt off like his own, and setting it down in the same spot, Lucas' eyes darting over for a moment, but Stephen flying a thumb to Lucas' chin, bringing focus back to brown eyes.

Button. Zipper. Fingers under waistband. Trousers and underwear slipping off, under a masterful touch.

Stephen discarding it all into the nothingness of the apartment, unimportant in the now.

He caresses touch over Lucas' ankles, to calves, behind knees, laying kisses as he explores his way to thighs, fingers tracing, lips enticing.

Lucas whimpers and moans, skin tingling, body glistening, heat rushing his brain, his untouched cock twitching, as his breath hitches.

Stephen inches closer and closer, but he's not there yet, and Lucas calls out, his voice reverberating around the apartment.

"P-please… S-Sir, please…"

But the only response, is fingers sinking into hot skin, and knavish eyes looking up into desperate ones, as Stephen pops up, silently commanding Lucas' sublime attention.

"A good slut is patient." Stephen asserts, dancing touches along Lucas' tie, his only remaining article of clothing. "Are you gonna be a good slut for me?"

Lucas nods. Small and emphatic. As though too much movement would spook an unseen force.

"Face down." Stephen says simply, grabbing one of the belts, folding it over itself.

A whimper escapes Lucas' lips, watching the brown leather in Stephen's dexterous grip, his mind a haze.

"Now." Stephen commands, snapping the belt forcefully.

Lucas scrambles onto his front, legs not cooperating, arms unsteady.

"No. Ass up. I can't have you grinding your dick on the couch."

A whimper vibrates through the couch, Lucas' face against the upholstery, keen and submissive.

He hears the jingle of a buckle, and feels his hands being gathered together behind his back, leather surrounding his wrists, moans reverberating along his cheek, neck, and shoulders, running up and down the fabric.

Stephen winds the belt around, once, twice, three times, threading the leather through the buckle, steady and focused.

Lucas replying with beautiful sounds, dazed eyes, and slight struggles against his restraints.

"Nuh-uh." Stephen retorts, fanning his fingers out, tracing touch up Lucas' arms, steadying the movements.

A delicious whimper floats from Lucas' plump lips, as he obeys, skin on fire under Stephen's touch.

He hears the other buckle, feels Stephen's fingers, running the leather over his nipples, and around his chest, as the strap is threaded through that buckle, securing his arms tight.

Glorious sounds fall from Lucas' lips, as he shifts slightly, wanting to feel just how helpless and bound he truly is. Beautiful. Desolate. Moreish.

Stephen traces his hands back down to Lucas' wrists, bringing lips to reddening palms, squirming under the belt, as he lays soft kisses on Lucas' hands. Exploring, slowly, purposefully, the curves of Lucas' palms, the tender skin, the peaks and valleys, his kisses moving along the fingers, and down to the small of Lucas' back.

A soft, low moan hums along the couch, Lucas shaking under Stephen's lips, overexcited and completely alight, the kisses sending salacious tingles up his spine, as he falls deeper into the ether.

Lips soft, kisses delicate, breath escaping with each move, Stephen traces the teases down, his fingers following, gentle touch in his kisses wake.

He pauses at the very edge of Lucas' back, taking a moment for his fingers to catch up to his mouth, as Lucas pleads, his words almost incoherent, floating over moans, dancing through his lips, muffling against the couch.

As Stephen grips his fingers into the soft flesh, his kisses become obscene, lips parting, tongue extending, teasing down a well-known path.

The room fills with the lustful moans of Lucas, as his anticipation reaches a fever pitch, his untouched cock twitches, and his skin glistens, as Stephen finally reaches his entrance.

"P-p...pl...please..." Lucas begs, lost in the overwhelming high.

Stephen is all too happy to comply, running his tongue along the sensitive ridges, hot breath highlighting his path.

Moans vibrate along the couch, as Lucas' arms shake, powerless in their restraints, as he is against the ecstasy rushing his system, every sensation heightened in his submissive state, bringing him to a new plane of existence with every tease.

Stephen squeezes, his fingers sinking into Lucas' soft arse, and releases, bringing one hand up, and back down hard, the flesh glowing vermilion.

The sting runs through Lucas like lightening, his entire body trembling, vulgar sounds pushing across his lips.

Stephen looks up, indulging in the sight of Lucas' shaking under him. Arms struggling against leather, back heaving and quivering, face absolutely crimson. Profane and dedicated.

He traces his tongue back up, slapping Lucas' other arsecheek, pausing for a beat.

"Can you handle more of this?" He speaks through Lucas' lewd moans

"Pl... P-please f-fuck m-me, S-Sir..." Lucas begs, his words broken by hot breaths and fiery moans.

Another hard slap rushing Lucas' system, his calves lifting and slamming back down in response.

"Oh, the bitch wants cock?" Stephen asks, rubbing lazy fingers over the redness he just caused.

A moan vibrates along the upholstery, desperate and wanting.

"I can't hear you." Stephen responds, slapping the other arsecheek, firm and commanding. "Speak clearer."

Without waiting for an answer, he grabs both cheeks again, and brings his face down, kissing and licking Lucas' entrance vigorously.

Vulgar sounds roar out of Lucas, as he's completely inundated with sanctity, his toes curling, his entrance pulsing, his cock dripping, the edge hanging just out of reach.

"Yellow!" He pushes out, the only word able to cut through his foggy mind.

That word hits Stephen instantly, even before it's fully left Lucas' mouth, it bolts into Stephen's brain.

He halts his kissing, and looks over Lucas, seeing an overstimulated body twitching and moaning.

Stephen's hot breath against Lucas' entrance sends powerful bolts of pleasure through his zealous form, as he tries to steady his own breath, and come down enough for form coherent words.

It's all calm. Not still, but placid. A respite in the glory of bliss.

Seconds stretch and pull, time slowing to a crawl, as they both settle back into the realm of the living.

"I... I wa-was g-getting too c-close, S-Sir..." Lucas pants.

The use of 'Sir' telling Stephen they were still in this, Lucas didn't want to stop, and neither did he.

"And I still have to fuck you." Stephen muses, lifting his face, and running his hands over Lucas' bound arms and glistening back.

"Y-yes... I w-want to be g-good..." Lucas agrees, keening into Stephen's touch. "P-please... Sir... please..."

Stephen answers by swiping the lube, Lucas hearing the sound of the cap opening, and Stephen squeezing the tube onto his fingers, the noises sending tingles up Lucas' spine, as he lay waiting and lustful.

With slick fingers, Stephen draws two down the crease, purposefully, soaking in the sounds emanating from Lucas.

He circles the ridges, deliberately, watching Lucas twitch and keen, and slowly, pushes inside, the walls pulsing around his fingers.

A strong moan glides up to Stephen, Lucas trying to push back, trying to take more, show how ready he is, how good he'll be for Stephen. Aching to please, lost and wanton.

Fingers leaving, a whine echoing, another finger added, pushing inside again, and a salacious noise hitting Stephen's ears, painting a roguish smile on his face.

His movements taking their time, enjoying every response from Lucas, stretching the moment into something otherworldly, as though it has no end and no beginning, it simply is, and always will be.

His other hand, leisurely tracing his very fingertips on the delicate surface of Lucas' overheated skin, along curves, over dips, exploring the shapes, delighting in the keening, the obscenity, the eagerness; as though Lucas has been drowning his whole life, and Stephen brought him up for air.

What a sacred gift, to help another feel safe enough to enjoy their own body.

"Pl... Please... S-Sir..."

Lucas' begging cuts through the trance, bringing Stephen back to the room, to solid ground, who knows how long he's been gone.

He slides his fingers out, Lucas trying to follow him, pushing back salaciously, hips high and desperate.

The rough fabric against his face, his arms restrained behind him, his neck crooked and twisting, the position should be painful, but he can't even register it. Somewhere, his body knows, but Lucas is drifting, missing to this world, entire body sunken deep into another dimension, all he can think of is finally feeling Stephen's cock push inside him, feeling Stephen's body against his, hands exploring his skin, consumed, wanted, taken.

Stephen slips off his briefs, cock hard and waiting, finally freed, wiping the slick off his fingers with the soft material, before tossing them somewhere in the abyss.

"Please... please, Sir..."

Lucas gets a firm arse-slap for his whines, as Stephen busies himself with rolling on a condom and reaching for more lube.

"Hold still, bitch."

Lucas doing as instructed, an eager plaything.

With one hand on Lucas' arsecheek, the other holding the tube high, Stephen aims droplets at Lucas' entrance, the muscles puckering in response, and another 'please' falling from Lucas' lips.

Stephen drips more lube along his cock, replacing the cap and setting the tube down, noticing Lucas watching his hand.

He brings his fingers up to Lucas' hair, tracing touches down the neck, along the spine, and over the soft arse, sinking grips into both cheeks.

Lucas tries to push back, but Stephen has those hips firmly in his grasp, and squeezes harder for emphasis, Lucas sinking into the couch, helpless and thrilled.

Stephen holds Lucas firm, lining himself up, and slowly, mercifully, eases his cock inside, moaning deeply, eager walls surrounding him. Transcendent pleasure flooding his system. Righteous communion.

A loud, obscene moan escapes Lucas, a man possessed, gone to the now, completely wrapped in the nirvana of forever.

"Th-th... thank y-you S-Sir..." He breathes, tied hands forming fists, feet lifting up, entire body consumed.

"Are you..." Stephen asks, hips moving back. "Gonna be..." thrusting forward. "A good little..." Back. "Slut for me?" Forward.

Sounds cascade from Lucas, none of them coherent, as he swims in the waters of ecstasy.

Unsatisfied with Lucas' answer, Stephen grabs Lucas' higher bind, and the back of his tie, and shifts them both back, Lucas suddenly on top, held completely by Stephen.

Relishing the heaven of dominance. Mind clear, body aflame, Lucas right where he loves to have him.

"I asked..." Growling into Lucas' ear. "Are you..." Hips grinding. "Gonna be..." Pulling Lucas' tie. "A good slut... for me?"

"Y-yes!" Lucas whimpers, voice straining, completely overwhelmed.

Stephen stills his hips, keeping his firm grip on the belt rubbing against Lucas's nipples, and his neck-squeezing tie, their bodies so close, sweat glistening.

"Then ride this dick, bitch."

Growling words causing pulses around Stephen's cock, as Lucas feels bolts of glory wash over him, inches from his own orgasm, as that good spot begs for friction, and his untouched cock twitches.

Lost completely, Lucas tries to move his hips, the awkward angle and fogged mind making it difficult, and he whines out into the apartment, frustrated at his own state.

Stephen watches the lewd display, Lucas oversexed and consumed by need, trying to grind his hips back, his desperation compounding.

It's sublime, Lucas completely given over to him, so alive and fervent. Absolute magic, ascending Stephen to a higher plane.

With grip firm, Stephen mercifully thrusts quick and rough, pulling on Lucas' tie, causing a majestic chorus from Lucas, building and amassing, mixing with his growls and moans.

And he stops. Lucas trying to grind back, failing miserably, as more beautiful sounds fall from cherry blossom lips.

"Oh, did you want me to keep fucking you?" Stephen teases, releasing Lucas' tie, head lulling forward.

Lucas tries to struggle against the belt around his chest, hoping to get more leverage, more friction, more anything, to quiet his screaming mind, fixating on only one thing.

"You don't? Ok, we can stop th-"

"No, pl-please!" Lucas calls, voice wrecked. "Pl-please keeping fu-fucking me, S-Sir, I n-need it s-so bad…"

Stephen hooks his arm around Lucas' throat, bringing ear to lips, nipping softly at Lucas's earlobe, and feeling walls pulse around his cock, enraptured in the sensation.

He squeezes. Counting into Lucas' ear.

"One… two… three…"

Releasing just enough for Lucas to catch his breath.

"You got that?"

Lucas keening, giving him an answer.

In one quick movement, Stephen pushes them forward, wrapping his other arm around Lucas' torso, surrounding Lucas completely.

Chest against back, arms tied between them, throat in the crook of an elbow, cock deep inside. The taken and the possessor.

Without warning, Stephen thrusts, hard and fast, squeezing his arm around Lucas' throat.

One...

Sounds building, layering, a chorus of sanctity.

Two...

Almost there, just a little more, they can both taste it.

Three...

He stops. Nothing but stillness. Lucas not daring to move.

Both breathless. Both so close. Both floating somewhere eternal.

"Are you... ready?" Stephen asks, tracing his hand down Lucas' torso, over hips, fingers closing around cock. "You gonna cum for me?"

"Y-yes... th-thank you!" Lucas keens, the intense pleasure of finally feeling fingers on his cock pulsing through him. "Y-yes pl-please, Sir!"

"Don't disappoint me, slut." Stephen growls, awash with the divinity of dominance, on the edge of release.

"I-I won't S-Sir!" Lucas whimpers, knowing his orgasm is a few thrusts away.

Stephen dances tantalising touches over the tip of Lucas' cock, eliciting moans that radiate from Lucas' back to his chest, vibrating through his body, inching him closer.

He grasps Lucas' cock firmly, and thrusts back slowly, feeling the ridges grip him, euphoric and heavenly.

Lucas keens and moans, ready and waiting, hoping to get his chance any second now.

And his hopes are answered.

Stephen thrusts rough and relentless, hitting that good spot, stroking that aching cock, covering Lucas completely, he can feel the edge, it's right there.

Moaning rough and vigorous into Lucas' ear, he squeezes his arm around Lucas' throat, feeling the gasping breaths against his skin; he has Lucas, engulfed in a concerto of shared moans, as his cock thrusts, against those walls that squeeze him. Almost.

"Now." Stephen grunts, deep and commanding, right into Lucas' ear.

It's all the warning Lucas needs, as his body spasms, flooding with delight, keening and moaning, ascending into the blessed plane, glorious and holy.

Stephen swims in it, Lucas cumming hard and quick, entire body shaking, chorus higher and urgent, yet deeper and free, and he feels it. Right there.

He calls out into the apartment, tightening his grip on Lucas' neck and cock, euphoria rushing, hips quivering, vision blurring, cum spilling, finding salvation.

The symphony of satisfaction seeps into every corner of the apartment, drab and minimal as the space may be, it is consecrated, holding such deliverance, such beauty, such joy.

Stephen floats down, a leaf falling from a tree in the soft autumn breeze, resting on the grass. His grips loosening, his breath steadying, as he stays here, basking in Lucas, indulging in a dream.

Gasping, Lucas comes to Earth, a fleck of snow, winding and curling, landing on the footpath, and completely dissolving. Sinking into the couch, absolutely spent, thankful for Stephen's embrace.

Stephen lays a soft kiss on Lucas' neck, simple and loving.

"You were so good for me."

"Thank you, Ste."

Part 26

Don't Pass Me Over

"Like, sure, Holly said it was gonna be eight or nine hours. But like, that was literally nine hours in a damn car." Stephen complains, stepping out of the rental, stretching, and looking up at the Palace Hotel. "But like, we did see a lot of the country, and we are here."

"I know, if you would've told teenage Lucas that he'd actually go to the hotel from 'Priscilla', I would've told you 'I'm not a fag, so fuck off!', so…" Lucas muses, nudging Stephen.

"I mean, you've never seemed like a fag to me." Stephen jokes, devious smile on his face. "It's like, a very heterosexual move to love giving blowjobs."

"It's probably the straightest thing I do." Lucas volleys, rounding the rental to grab their bags out of the boot.

"Like, I know you're joking, but every time you had the aux, you were blasting the faggiest music in the world." Stephen retorts, leaning against the car, and playfully shrugging.

"So, now you don't support women?" Lucas returns, plopping their bags on the ground, and closing the boot.

"I support women, but it's like... Lu, it was a lot of Kylie Minogue." Stephen replies, holding back a smile. "And the fact I know it was Kylie Minogue, means I totally support women. I mean, like, I usually support them on my face, but..."

"Ok, but let's be genuine, you don't listen to any women." Lucas throws back, light-hearted, with hands on hips. "You just kept playing that whiny emo band."

"Wait, wait, wait." Stephen defends, holding up palms, face impish. "That was because you said you'd never heard The Wonder Years, and I do think their music works best in the context of a full album."

Stephen punctuates his point with a mine of adjusting invisible glasses, and a look faux-defiance.

"So, you don't support women's albums." Lucas jokingly debates, nodding like he's in a pantomime. "I see how it is."

"I would've played you all of 'Reputation', if you hadn't already heard that one." Stephen protests, looking to the sky in put-on indignation, and back to Lucas, face full of adoration.

"I just think you should advocate for women that *aren't* Taylor Swift." Lucas shrugs, pouting his bottom lip and raising his eyebrows, a cunning little shit.

"You literally said that you didn't want to listen to Evanescence because it was too heavy, and you didn't want to listen to Mitski because it was too sad."

Stephen protests, delighted annoyance moving through his words. "You need to pick a crime."

"Oh, so *all of a sudden* liking women in pop music is a crime." Lucas protests, speaking with an air of a lawyer giving their closing argument. "Well, lock me up for enjoying the Sugababes and-"

"Ok, but didn't you say yourself that they rotate the babes every six months?" Stephen interrupts, pointing expectedly at Lucas.

"So now we're calling women babes?" Lucas points out, feigning shock.

"You're literally so ridiculous." Stephen shakes his head, smirk poking through his exasperation. "Can we please just go in?"

"And I supposed you want me to carry the bags." Lucas retorts, reaching for their luggage, with a put-on huff. "For I am a lowly working-class boy?"

"You're literally older than me." Stephen protests, delight poking through his words. "And you *know* I'm from Philly, and not the cushy suburbs, like..."

"All I'm hearing is reasons why you don't support women." Lucas remarks, pouting and heading for the check-in.

"You're totally ridiculous." Stephen laughs, following.

The clerk checks them in without comment, no need for some kind of 'yes and' exercise, about two men booking the one-bedroom Priscilla Boudoir, thankfully. And the pair take a moment to drink in the gorgeous murals, before heading up, setting down bags, and looking around their room.

"They said it was 'just like the movie' but..."

"It genuinely is." Lucas interrupts, looking to Stephen with unbridled joy.

"It is!" Stephen delights, bringing his palms to his temples, eyes flitting all around.

Lucas takes a different approach, inspecting every element, exploring the room with curious wonder, equalling enthralled by the bathroom fixtures and the gorgeous artworks, with a loud gasp escaping his lips when he notes where the doors lead.

"Th-the... you got the... with the...?" Lucas stumbles, pointing to the balcony, and turning to Stephen with absolute glee.

"Yeah, it's a shared area, but..." Stephen muses, sauntering over, wrapping his arms around Lucas' waist. "We can sit out there, watch the sunset..."

Lucas looks into warm brown eyes, feeling so wooed, so considered. Stephen really is always thinking of him, in a million little ways, hoping to surprise him, to romance him, to carve out moments of significant insignificance, the kinds of gestures that can be so easily overlooked, if someone doesn't know how to see them.

He leans down slightly, laying a soft kiss on Stephen's lips. A gesture of 'thank you', of 'I appreciate this', as the words themselves once again sit just outside of Lucas' reach.

Stephen smiles up at Lucas, hearing him loud and clear.

"I'm glad you like it." He replies modestly, standing on his tip-toes to reach up, and lay a response kiss on Lucas' nose. "But I did see a few reviews mention the thin walls, so I'll have to get the ball-gag out for you."

"Silencing me again." Lucas jokingly protests. "I see what this relationship has become."

"Whatever." Stephen replies, rolling his eyes, smile on his lips. "You wanna go out and watch the sunset or not?"

Lucas completely softens, his faux-indignation gone in an instant, and they head out into the warm April late afternoon, the sky already shifting from brightest azure to soft lavender, melting into vibrant amber and striking, scorching gold.

They shuffle some chairs, and settle in, watching the colours shift and melt minute to minute, as the street below bustles, with its wide roads, small businesses, and desert charm, an opal in the red dust.

The sunset turns to twilight, and into dusk, as the pair watch, present and slow, such a contrast to their bustling days, endless meetings, and phone calls to foreign offices.

To breathe in the changing of the sky, what wondrous respite.

Ancient and modern, for humans have always enjoyed sunsets, moonlight, sunrises, and burning sun, through destructive wars and personal turmoil, as the world turns and it feels futile to wish, hope, and dream, the sky will always change, will always stay the same, another cloudy day, another midnight, no two alike, and yet, always present.

And to share such beauty with another? What a gift.

Part 27

I Actually Hate Emails!

From: Susan Leung <sleun@holmsyorke.com>
Sent: Friday, 26 April 2019 09:16 AM
To: Stephen Herzig <sherz@holmsyorke.com>
Subject: FW: Melbourne Contract SH 543-972

Morning Stephen,

Please find attached details of your contract,
which won't be renewed in the new financial year.

Any questions, let me know.

Cheers,

Susan Leung (she/her)
Human Resource Senior Manager
Holms & Yorke Bank Melbourne

Part 28

So, I Guess We Just Keep Driving With The Weight Of This Information

The days came and went, a blur of joys large and little, moments caught in the net of time. Sex that attempts to keep quiet, hot and vigorous. Walks around a town coated in a heat-haze, even as the Autumn tries, and fails, to set in. Sunrises and art gazing, sleeping in and drag performances, laying together and desert sculptures.

Like stepping into another dimension, a stunning place to get lost in the now.

But, as with so many wonders, it must come to an end.

A thud as Lucas loads their bags in the boot, felt by Stephen as he sits in the driver's seat, scrolling through his downloaded music, looking for something Lucas might enjoy.

He decides on a playlist Holly sent him, a mix of Australian dance tunes and pop rock, to get him schooled on the music of his temporary home.

Pressing play as Lucas opens the passenger door, he's met with a smile, as Lucas beams.

"The Veronicas? From whence did this woman-supporting fag emerge?"

"He's been right here, baby." Stephen retorts, bobbing along to the thick, synth bassline of 'Hook Me Up'. "All I needed was this trusty playlist."

"Alright, well, I'll just wait and see." Lucas jokes, nodding along, beaming. "This is only the first song."

Stephen playfully shakes his head, pulling the rental away, glancing at Lucas once more before heading down the wide streets of Broken Hill, playlist blaring.

Minutes stretch and pull away from them, as they drive along the barren roads, the Autumn sun beating down in the late April morning, blazing before ten a.m., as though the Summer sinks it's claws into the red earth here, unrelenting and overpowering, creating a sense of timelessness, the seasons running together into one state, a miracle and a misfortune.

The journey back ebbs and flows, with comfortable silence, playful and genuine conversation, and various genres of tunes, all playing equal parts in the overture of the hours.

Stretching, glorious planes hugging them, as scrubs freckle and sprinkle, and trees speck and scatter, until the barren sprawling land, gives way to greenery, and the pair know they're nearing Melbourne.

"Probably a good time to turn off Airplane Mode." Stephen muses, picking up his phone.

"Turn off what?" Lucas teases, shooting a quick smile from the driver's side.

"This is bullying, I'm being bullied." Stephen retorts, with put-on offence.

"I just want you to tell me what the mode is again." Lucas playfully continues.

"I'm gonna turn off *Aeroplane* Mode." Stephen responds, eyes rolling, smiling. "Are you happy with that? Is that ok?"

"Yes, I am." Lucas shrugs, playful smile curling as he focuses on the road. "I just think you should use words that are correct."

"Sometimes I think you're worse than Holly." Stephen razes, grinning.

"Hey! Don't say that. We're both equally horrible." Lucas retorts, laughing to himself, before continuing. "It doesn't have to be a competition, just because you put your knob in both of us."

"I mean, if you must know, I never- shit!" Stephen interrupts himself, seeing quite possibly the most unwanted work email to ever exist.

Lucas notices the complete shift in a singular syllable, and indicates, changing lanes, and pulling off the Citylink, into the shoulder. Hazard lights clicking, with the murmur of Fall Out Boy's 'Church' easing through the stereo, and the whooshing of cars passing them by.

The pair sitting for a moment in the odd mix of low sounds.

"So... my contract didn't get renewed." Stephen begins again, his tone as deflated as his body. "I'm here until thirty June, like, not here, but..."

Lucas nods, seen by Stephen in his peripheral vision, as the suddenly sunk Stephen stares forward, focusing on the dashboard.

"Two months." Stephen states, zoned-out and processing, trying to comprehend the information. "Just two months."

Again, Lucas nods, words escaping his grasp.

"Like it's nothing, like I'm nothing, but... fuck, why am I surprised?" Stephen laments, leaning deep into the seat, eyes closing.

Lucas looks over to his love, unsure how to respond, the tools that Stephen has, so evasive to him.

"I don't... I'm sorry... I'm, um... not sure..." He stumbles, looking over Stephen's defeated form, unseen by closed eyes.

Stephen looks over to him, eyes weary, half-smile willing its way onto lips, considering him. He's not one for words, but by the grace of these Greater Melbourne clouds, he is trying.

"Thanks." Stephen replies, reaching an open hand over the turbulent waters of the centre console.

Lucas takes the hand, a bridge over rushing rivers.

"I love you." He says, the words falling out with ease, as though they carry no weight.

Stephen's eyes widening, almost disbelieving that not only is Lucas the first to say those three words, but that they haven't shared this yet, in sixteen storied months.

"Fuck, I shouldn't have said that." Lucas deflates, looking out the windshield at the speeding cars, hand still in loveable hand. "Not that I don't mean it, but... um... this is an awful time to-"

"I love you, too." Stephen interrupts, the words leaving his lips effortlessly as well, a truth known, but only now spoken.

"Well, fuck."

"Yeah... fuck."

How a silence seeps in, even with the clicking, the cars, and the music. As the tracks tick over, belting vocals and doo-wop instrumentals swarming the stereo, purple essence filing in, a mix of everything and anything that hurts, the lyrics hitting Stephen like they're new, because in some ways, they are. He's never been here before, and it's scary as all hell.

And in the dying hours, resolution is found.

"I mean, look, it's like, this way we do have a chance to, like, actually cherish this time, like, while we have it." Stephen speaks into the car, 'Heaven's Gate' murmuring in background. "You get me?"

"Yeah... yeah I do." Lucas replies, squeezing Stephen's hand, trying to push strong emotions down, even as he's equally trying to fight such a compulsion.

"Ok... like, we're gonna have the best two months, like, while we can." Stephen agrees, his voice cracking under the weight of tears sitting just under the surface. "And... like, how about... you stay at my place... tonight, this weekend, whatever."

Lucas just nods, wiping away a tear he couldn't keep in.

A shared breath, Lucas waiting for a clear run, and joining the traffic, the music alone, their only reprieve from the quiet. Neither turning it up, it continues whispering, low and unintrusive, as the album melts time, and they reach the rental drop-off.

It's all business for a brief, merciful, respite. Something they both know well, a familiar atmosphere, of forms and payment cards, identification and signatures. But soon it's done, and they're not yet home free.

Pulled so tight, they might snap at any minute, they wait in silence for the rideshare, sit in silence in the back, for a journey that pressed on temples and hammered down on chests. A battle to remain composed.

Until finally, they arrive, a small grace, almost. They still have to make it through the lobby, and up to that front door, time being unkind, and seconds pulling into unrelenting eternities.

Each breath stabbing daggers into lungs, as he shakes, key in hand, reaching, hoping, as the lock resists, another obstacle.

And insistent, it won't turn, Stephen collapsing, unable to hold it all in. Tears streaming, rivers of misery, as he curls around his duffle bag, against the door, defeated by the day.

Lucas bobs down with him, arm around the man who has always radiated patience, is ever understanding, given Lucas every courtesy, now cracked, and showing it, not just to Lucas, but to anyone who might pass by. No longer having the energy to hold it off.

Stephen can't stay here, he pushes the key to Lucas, weeping and wordless.

Lucas unlocks the door, and thinks better of opening it, with a tearful Stephen leaning into it. He squats down, arm under Stephen's, and lifts them both, swinging open the threshold to privacy.

Guiding Stephen inside, he helps him down onto his own lowline couch, in his near-identical company apartment, carbon copies of the most drab idea of a living space, all white, some grey, and the least amount of colour possible, plus no one can make any changes, or their contracts will be terminated. Though now that was a reality, a loud voice inside

Stephen urged him to destroy every fucking surface in this place, leaving it a hollow shell, just as he felt now.

Lucas leaves Stephen on the couch, dipping back out to retrieve their bags, and grabbing Stephen's keys, before gently closing the door, with a slight click.

He joins Stephen on the couch, their bodies intertwining, seeking comfort, confirmation the other is here, in this reality, on this plane of existence.

Cheeks red, with no idea of when he started crying, feeling his head throb, but he's not moving, he seeks only to live in Stephen's arms. In any way, for any time, please.

Stephen pulling him in closer, tears soaking into casual tees, and cascading down onto the baby blue couch, as the harmony of grief fills the apartment, intimacy in sorrow.

Part 29

I Actually Don't Wanna Be A Part Of It, Babes

Clothes discarded, hands exploring, breath hot.

Stephen pulls him in, kissing him intense and slow, lips laced with sadness, yet acceptance, trying desperately to get one last taste.

Lucas pulls back, so unlike him.

"Can we... not? Just, maybe... lay here instead?" He asks, eyes elusive.

"Of course." Stephen responds, smiling softly, waiting for Lucas to return his gaze. "I'd love to."

Lucas sees Stephen. Eyes meeting eyes, studying faces, taking note, digesting, remembering, here and now.

Stephen guides them down, naked on his bed, facing, exposed, unguarded.

Open and inviting in a way Lucas always tries to be, as he pushes past layers of lies, echoing inside him, of what a man should be.

Regret lacing his studying gaze, trying his best to take in every part of Stephen's face, snapping a mental picture for when their time runs out in the morning.

The beauty mark just above Stephen's cupid's bow, ever inviting Lucas' lips, the faint freckles that peek through his olive skin, spreading from the apples of his cheeks, to the very bridge of his nose, always showing the time of year, as they bold and fade, the chestnut and amber layers of his eyes, deep and warm, Lucas' greatest comfort or his largest hesitance.

Stephen is feeling it, the intensity of Lucas' eyes on him, watching him in a manner he'd usually watched Lucas, but with such different intentions. Desire, heartache.

The slight lines on Lucas' forehead, ridged in concern, his eyes evergreen and yearning, when of course he is deciduous, ever changing, yet rooted in his ways, as much as he fought against himself. The cherry blossom of his full lips muted, as he purses them, draining the colour, more comfortable, this time, in watching, and not in being watched.

Stephen reaches up to push a tuff of Lucas' salt-and-pepper hair off those forehead lines, his laugh lines showing themselves instead, his dimples following, and his lips regaining some soft colour, his smile returning at Stephen's touch. His cheeks giving him away too, blushing pink under pale skin, no hiding his feelings.

What glorious freedom, to lay bare with another, and look over them, with love, with wonder, with a hope to perceive. In complete silence, without bias, no hope other than to take the vision of them in absolutely.

And what excruciating pain, to know this is because tomorrow one of you is leaving, and the clock is ticking.

"I..." Lucas tries, his words evasive.

"I love you too." Stephen answers, knowing Lucas' words exactly.

"I... w-wish..." Lucas tries again, his voice cracking, his eyes welling.

"Me too." Stephen affirms, reaching up to wipe away a tear, as it travels down Lucas' face.

Lucas buries his head in the pillow, streams of salt escaping his eyes, and calls of anguish hiding in the material.

A hand from Stephen, well of course, fingers tracing over Lucas's temple, along his ear, down his neck, to his chest, palm resting on heart.

Stephen's eyes closing, feeling the beat, breathing it all in. The grief, the intimacy, the love.

Tears spilling and time passing, as it always will, unstoppable by mere human hopes. Stephen covering them in his large, soft, duvet, warming them against the chilling winter seeping in.

Two months flying by, and one last night spent mostly awake, willing every second to count, hoping to catch every last moment, and store it somewhere both unreachable and unbreakable, in the most secure place.

Ready and waiting to be recalled at any time, on the most crisp screen, and remind them both that this is genuine and true. It can never be taken or erased, as much as it has to end here and now.

How the morning rolls in, powerful and inescapable, and of course it's a fucking Monday.

Alarm cutting through the air, harsh and unwanted, stating a truth known in their bones.

A sleepless night written on both their faces, eyes puffy, with hundreds of red lines running through the whites, stinging on every blink. Cheeks sullen and faded, Lucas' bright blush, usually so vivid, almost unseen. Lips too, colour-drained. Death warmed up.

But they both smile, equally glad to have spent their last night seeing each other so truly, unphased by their changing faces in the cold morning.

Stephen closes the gap, pressing his skin to Lucas, arms around bodies, fading into each other, one final time.

It's Lucas who lifts his head, trying to catch Stephen's lips, drinking in a passionate kiss, tongues massaging, profound and honest. Desire and dejection.

But it's short-lived, as a bing informs a text message, stating a company car is twenty minutes away.

Stephen checks the sound, knowing it won't be good news, and informs Lucas, who bounces up, throwing on last night's clothes, and turning to see if he can be of any help.

But being Stephen, he's all ready, enough space in his open, packed, suitcase for yesterday's clothes, duffle by the door, and today's ensemble ready and waiting, he grabs the pile, and heads to the bathroom.

"Anything I can do?" Lucas asks, instinctively following Stephen as he goes.

"Just give me a sec, then come keep me company?" Stephen requests, placing his pile down on the edge of the bathtub, and turning to a waiting Lucas.

He nods, closing the door, and heading back into the bedroom, kneeling down next to the open suitcase, he spots something in Stephen's clear toiletry bag that gives way to pause.

Roll-on tea tree oil deodorant.

The brand he wears. An attempt to embrace his new home. Fragrant. Unique. Reflected back at him by Stephen.

Wiping away a bittersweet tear, he zips up the vibrant chartreuse suitcase, and brings it to the front door, joining the duffle. He leans precariously on the arm of Stephen's baby blue couch, staring at the symbols of travel and change, trying to keep new tears from his reddened eyes.

Lucas is shaken from his thoughts, as he hears the toilet flush, and Stephen calling to him from the bathroom.

He wonders over, letting himself in, sitting next to the folded clothes, silently watching Stephen.

Smiling up at him, Lucas is entranced, Stephen catching Lucas' eye in the mirror, as he washes his face, Lucas lost in the beauty of the mundane, and thankful to simply have him here, even through the painful haze of so little sleep, and the crushing anguish of time ticking down.

"The deodorant?" Lucas asks, smiling as tears well.

"Hmm?" Stephen responds, wetting the washcloth again, and wiping down his pits and bits. "The what?"

"Tea tree deodorant." Lucas states, salt escaping his eyes.

"Oh." Stephen getting it, turning, naked and seen. "Yeah... I, like, wanted to grab some... in case I can't get it back home, like..."

"It's the same one?" Lucas follows, unable, even now, to speak directly.

"Yeah... to remind me..." Stephen affirms, bobbing down in front of Lucas, hands on his knees, eyes warm.

Lucas smiles, droplets cascading down his cheeks, Stephen reaching up to wipe them away, nodding.

Wordlessly communicating a thousand affirmations, sitting in the moment with Lucas.

Another bing floods panic into Stephen's eyes, standing, and reaching for the pile of clothes, Lucas getting up to check.

He races to the bedroom, seeing the text noting the car is delayed, and giving a new arrival time.

"You've got ten minutes!" He calls from the bedroom, jogging into the bathroom, and showing Stephen the screen.

He pokes his head through his t-shirt and a huffs a sigh of relief, but knows he hasn't been bought much time.

Throwing on the rest of his clothes, he heads for the door, Lucas following, as they both don their shoes, and Stephen notices the suitcase.

"You zipped it up and brought it out?" Stephen asks, looking from the suitcase to Lucas.

"Is… is that ok?" Lucas nervously questions, looking to his feet.

"Yeah, it's very thoughtful."

Stephen leans in for a chaste kiss, taking extra pause, and leaning forehead against forehead, speaking a sonnet without words.

Another bing. The car's outside. This is it.

He locks the door. They head down. Glass doors open. A waiting black car.

One last hug, eyes slamming shut, hoping to take just a little more for the road, deep breaths, tired minds, heartbreaking and distinct.

They separate, green eyes looking into brown ones, stinging, even in the soft winter light, a squeeze of the arm, a gesture to open the boot, a bag, then suitcase, in the back, Stephen in the seat, a wave as he's driven away.

A man alone on the street. One more in a car. Just another July morning to everyone else.

Part 30

This House Is Full Of Ghosts

How the days melted together, buttons of chocolate over boiling water, no longer their own pieces, now one alloy unto itself.

Lucas looks over his minimalist apartment. Soulless. Replica of a facsimile bullshit. He resents this space. Not only for its narrowing walls, but for its memories. How their painful stings sink into his skin, boring through his veins, on nights like this.

Sink full of mugs, most still with green tea bags, one of his many attempts at health, and distance from his homeland, while still fitting into a deep-running routine. For pushing a boulder up the hill, just for it to roll back down, is still progress, even if he's the only one who knows it.

But oh, December. Finally, an approaching, merciful end, to a year he often felt he'd never escape. And he should be hopeful, he should even be excited.

For tomorrow, on the same phone with which he constantly tries to distract himself, he'll see the face he misses like nothing else.

Memories burning into his brain, ghosts surrounding his happiness and suffocating it. How he would've done things differently if he'd only known.

And oh, how he often came to that agonising conclusion.

He looks over the couch. Low line, muted yellow, the only thing in this fucking apartment with any colour. Not that he'd change much if he could. Wrapping around the living area, pointing to the flatscreen TV, a grey coffee table in between.

Stephen was there. He was right there. So many times. Like it was nothing, like it isn't moving mountains, walking on water, reviving the dead.

No. Back then it felt like the easiest thing in the world, the most natural phenomenon.

Lounging in his white briefs and one of Lucas' grey t-shirts, the afternoon sun streaming in, bright and blazing, illuminating him, a blessing personified. At ease, talking about how there's no heaven, except the one we make here, for ourselves and the ones we love.

And he pauses, he looks to Lucas, feeling seen. Because of course Lucas is just watching him, stopped in tracks, tray in hand.

He laughs and jokes, attempts at shaking his embarrassment, Lucas continuing to simply soak him in. Unable to get enough. And what else is new.

That Summer break was magic. He practically lived here, wearing Lucas' clothes, toothbrush in the cup, buying groceries for the two of them, domestic and effortless.

One of many ghosts.

Like Stephen laying with Lucas, head on Lucas' chest, absolutely tearing apart the film they just watched, face alight, as his mouth moves a mile a minute, and his eyes roll with every third word. Absolute beauty.

One hand gesturing exuberantly, the other pinned between them, held hostage in the heat of his monologue, as he points out the lazy cinematography and its effect on the storytelling, Lucas drinking him in like a favourite beverage.

So animated, completely carried away, showing yet another facet of himself to Lucas.

An absolute treat, to feel secure enough to turn slightly, and have the light hit differently, saying: 'this is another side, do you still accept me?'

Spirits, visions, apparitions.

Like fucking slowly, the July winter bringing a muted light, flooding the entire apartment in a haze, like floating through clouds.

Lucas rolling his head back, Stephen's hands holding firmly, as thighs straddle thighs, hips grind against hips, and waves of pleasure assemble, accumulate.

Stephen guiding him forward, stay with me, hands exploring up his back, lips trying to find his, tongues meeting, breath hot, as he grinds down, hitting the glorious spot.

Time melting away, an eclipse, heavenly and momentary, existing for a blip. How wondrous to be fleeting.

But to be here. To be now. What a tremendous weight. What a harrowing reality to be surrounded all day, every day, by the reminders of what was shared here, what lived here, what will never be here again.

Part 31

Video Chats With My Boo?
NOT CLICKBAIT)!!

There he is.

He looks healthier. Eyes brighter. But not too much.

After all, it hasn't been that long, or so the calendar says.

Lucas waves silently at him, hopeful and vigorous.

"Can you hear me?" Lucas asks, concerned that Stephen's silence was a technical glitch.

"Oh, yeah... Yeah, I can hear you!" Stephen beams back. "Can you hear me?"

"Yeah. Y-yeah, I can... Loud and clear."

A pause fills the call. Two men looking at pixelated approximations of each other. Feeling the physical and emotional distance.

"Y-you... look good." Stephen stumbles, gently clearing the silence, a softness in his eyes.

"Thank you, Ste." Lucas replies, tears pooling as he smiles, bittersweet. "You look good. Healthy and bright."

"Aww, Lu!" Stephen smiles, hand over his heart, just in frame. "That's very kind. I've been feeling it, but trying to keep... like, alive or something, I don't know."

"It's working." Lucas says simply, smile small but present. "It's so nice to see you... well, y'know."

Stephen beams, lifting his shoulders, pressing one cheek against his thick, warm, winter jumper.

"It's been... too long." He says, brow furrowing, head tilting. "I'm sorry about rescheduling, the time difference is... tough... and like, the holidays, but... I'm sorry."

"I'm sorry too. But it's so good to be here now." Lucas replies, feeling tears fall, and hands shaking.

"Oh, Lu..." Stephen consoles, reaching toward the screen, and miming wiping away a tear. "Cry all you need. I'd hold you if I was there."

"A-and I'd h-hold you right b-back." Lucas stammers, his voice uneven as salt streams down his hot cheeks. "Fuck! I miss you."

"I miss you too." Stephen nods, eyes sincere, temple leaning on his knuckles, watching Lucas. "I do, Lu. I miss you."

Lucas forces a smile through tears, nodding vigorously, trying to look at the moving image of Stephen, hoping he, himself, doesn't look too wrecked in pixels.

"C-can we t-talk about so-something else?" Lucas requests, feeling all-too-seen, if only by phone camera.

"Yeah totally!" Stephen declares, considering for a moment, opening his mouth a few times, before deciding on hopefully a better topic. "Any... nah, that's terrible... ok... are you seeing anyone?"

Lucas can't hide it. His entire face falling, unpleasant surprise running through him, eyes wide.

"What?" He asks weakly.

"No? Lockdown's got that, like, off the table?" Stephen follows up, curious and light.

"A-are you... seeing s-someone...?" Lucas asks, trying with every cell in his body to not let more tears fall. Not on this call.

Stephen avoids the watchful eye of the camera, looking off in different directions, giving an answer before even speaking.

"Yes."

"Ok." Lucas responds, leg bouncing under the kitchen island, unseen by the camera, or Stephen.

"We can... talk about this." Stephen states, calm, but clearly shaken. "Would you like to do that?"

"I dunno, Ste." Lucas replies, looking up, hoping that'll keep him from crying, Midlands accent thickening, as he feels perceptive eyes on him. "This is feeling like a session, and you're not Dawn, y'know? I don't... I don't want to feel like your patient."

"I get that. I hear you."

"It's just... you don't miss me?" Lucas asks, shame flooding him at feeling so needy.

"Lu, I miss you. I'll probably miss you for the rest of my life." Stephen affirms, hugging himself, cosy in his winterwear. "And... I'm seeing someone new. Those two things are true, for me."

"Ok. I don't wanna say anything else because I'll sound stupid." Lucas states, embarrassment flashing hot, even in the aircon of his modern apartment.

"You won't. It's just you and me. No one else is here." Stephen reassures, Philly accent lacing his words, warmer still. "But also, if you're not ready to tell me something, that's ok too. You know?"

Lucas nods, curt and quick.

Stephen lets the silence settle, still feeling an ease in shared quiet with Lucas.

He smiles to himself, remembering the last night they spent together, in person, feeling this is somehow similar, and yet, painfully different.

Lucas looks to Stephen, watching that smile, a smile sunken into his brain, living there, ready to soothe him whenever he could need.

"It's just... I miss you so much..." Lucas confesses, knowing he's free here, this is a sacred space. "And I can't imagine seeing someone else, when you're... you're still so present in my... I dunno... system or something."

Stephen soaks in Lucas' words, allowing them to really be absorbed, looking to Lucas with those sincere, brown eyes.

"I hear that. That's fucking real." Stephen affirms, nodding slowly. "I definitely can miss you and then also, like, be interested in someone else, so if that's not as natural for you... Yeah, it's gonna feel... like a betrayal. But I'm not trying to hurt you."

"What are you trying to do?" Lucas questions, eyes not daring to meet the screen.

"Wow. That's sorta a big question." Stephen ponders, taking in a heavy breath, and looking to his ceiling. "I guess it's like... if I only sit in the darkness, it'll swallow me whole, and maybe I'll never come out. And compounding onto that, being back at home, it's like, all this stuff I missed, and... like, plenty I don't. Am I making sense?"

"Yeah." Lucas nods, flicking nervous glances.

"Yeah, so it's like..." Stephen continues, guilt racing through his veins, words coming slow. "As much as I... cherish you, and like, I **loved** being in Melbourne with you, and like... like, I still hold onto you, in some ways, it's like... like, I need to also be... open to someone new, and I've... sorta readapted to, like, American life, or I think I'd... like, lose my mind."

"Ok." Lucas manages, hoping to note that he's listening, but not necessarily agreeing.

"And... not to be harsh, but... it's like, it *has* been a year..." Stephen continues, catching his own mistake, the time sitting in his system differently. "And a half! Like, a year and a half, sorta like... that's a while, like... and the whole thing going on... and like, we also, like... never really said, sorta... like, how we were gonna move forward. Am I making sense?"

Lucas nods. Unable to bring words out, but hoping to show Stephen he is trying to take them in.

"Are you alright?" Stephen checks, his brow furrowing in genuine concern.

"I w-will be. Um, I mean... e-everything you say is, y'know, true..." Lucas manages, pushing with every fibre of his body to get these words out, and along the cables running along the bottom of the ocean. "And as usual... you're, um... putting it in s-such a nice way... it's just... um, I think I was h-hoping for, um... something that I never... y'know... um, actually spoke to you about."

"I hear that." Stephen half-smiles, breathing Lucas' words in. "And I appreciate that, like, you're open to what I'm saying."

Lucas tenses, many warring impulses ripping and clawing their way to be heard, to pilot the flaming plane. He glances to Stephen, waiting in sweet sincerity, and knows which will take the controls as this flight goes down.

"Still hurts though." He laments, trying to push a smile to soften the blow, to whom, he's unsure.

"Yeah." Stephen agrees, seeing the battle all over Lucas' face. "Unfortunately, there's... like, not so much I can do about that, like, not from all the way over here... Except, like, do you wanna just sit in silence for a while?"

"Th-that would be... r-really nice."

How the quiet returns. Familiar. Comfortable. Slipping through the cracks of reality, and into a space without reverberating feedback, where only the truest noise comes through: silence.

Lucas looks over the approximation of Stephen, he does look good. It's almost annoying, like this year hasn't touched him, at least on the outside. Perhaps it's this new someone, perhaps it's all that catharsis he constantly seeks, perhaps he's just more resilient than Lucas.

It stings, to think others are just coded differently, breathing into stronger cells, more capable of healing. Or maybe it's learned, a puzzle Lucas hasn't yet been able to solve.

Stephen takes Lucas in, his moving image not doing him any justice. He looks older, far more than he should. Like time has sped up for him. In Melbourne. Without Stephen. A year in which he was fighting against himself.

The guilt pangs, maybe he should've offered more to Lucas, been more present in the past eighteen months. But the year changed him too, stock was taken of all that he gave to Lucas, in the end, to his own detriment.

Of course, he doesn't regret their time together. For they were like cherry blossoms in the spring, breathtaking and glorious, timing was everything, location was more. And quietly, the chapter has been closed in his mind for some time.

"Can I ask a question?" Lucas pipes up, shaking Stephen from his musings.

"Anything." Stephen graciously answers, remorse smarting, hoping to repent.

"What do you mean by..." Lucas tries, barely able to look at Stephen, feeling foolish for wanting more from this man. "By… adapting to American life? Are you… shooting rifles or something?"

Stephen tries to hold in a chortle, but failing is his burden right now, the sound escaping, and his following words swooping in as best they can.

"No, no, no. Not at all." He replies, putting on his best I-can-see-why-you'd-assume-that face. "It's more… like, it's time with my family, and practicing again, and like… Oh! I mean, I got to see The Wonder Years in Philly again. And that gig was right before everything, it was like the literal day before. Sorta… eerie, now I think about it."

"And you couldn't go to live music here?" Lucas follows up, trying to sneak glances.

Stephen considers the question, debating if he should be honest, and to what degree.

"I mean… I couldn't see The Wonder Years at The Fillmore… and it's like… like, I was trying to… sorta assimilate or something… I went to Rush with Holly, like… I called my family when I could but like… time difference is a bitch, and you know that… and I… like, sorta stopped practicing, which I… have weird feelings about."

Lucas sat in Stephen's words, running along the wires, funnelling directly into his brain, and soaking into the tired flesh.

"Ok." Lucas replies meekly. "Thanks."

"I feel like it's not okay."

"It is." Lucas lies, eyes on his lap, hoping to move on from this sting quickly. "What else have you been up to?"

Stephen considers for a moment, knowing Lucas is being evasive for a reason. But of course, this is not his garden, not his flowers. He can't tend to everyone every time.

He answers, speaking of the election aftermath, festive plans, and the fast-approaching new year.

Lucas nods along, willing himself to listen, for his mind to not wonder, not now, with Stephen somewhere in his presence.

What a harrowing reality, to taste the progress on your tongue, to will yourself to change, and still look at your feet sinking in the quicksand of your own hurt.

Part 32

Qwote Msngr, Online ⬤

Sunday, 07 July 2019 09:59

Ready 😇

> *Stephennnn video called you 10:01*
>
> 56mins

Sunday, 14 July 2019 09:59

ready👀?

> yep!!

You video called Stephennnn

59mins

Sunday, 21 July 2019 10:00

Readyyy👀

> *Stephennnn video called you 10:02*
>
> 58mins

Monday, 29 July 2019 08:09

How was fam time? ♡

> great!! happeing
>
> it's 6pm sun here u?

Good. Looking forward
to next week 😇

> me too!! 😵

You 👍 this message 08:14

Friday, 02 August 2019 09:52

> sorry!! can't do this week after all
>
> more family time 😊
>
> next week?

Ok. I hope you enjoy.

Stephennnn 👍 this message 9:59

Sunday, 11 August 2019 09:58

Ready???

> *Stephennnn video called you 09:58*
>
> 57mins

Sunday, 08 September 2019 09:59

Readyyyyy

Stephennnn video called you 09:59

59mins

Sunday, 27 October 2019 09:57

Readyy👀

Stephennnn video called you 09:58

52mins

Sunday, 08 December 2019 09:59

rrrrrready😇

Stephennnn video called you 10:00

59mins

Wednesday, 01 January 2020 16:05

Happy New Year 🎉

woo haaaappy neeeew yeeeear!!!!

Stephennnn video called you 17:48

16mins

Sunday, 16 February 2020 10:01

ready nowww

Stephennnn video called you 10:03

1hr 19mins

Sunday, 22 March 2020 10:48

Stephennnn video called you 10:48

37mins

Wednesday, 25 March 2020 08:29

readyyyy 📲

Stephennnn video called you 08:30

26mins

Saturday, 28 March 2020 09:59

Stephennnn video called you 09:59

1hr 07mins

Tuesday, 31 March 2020 08:30

readd 📲

Stephennnn video called you 08:31

27mins

Sunday, 05 April 2020 09:59

Stephennnn video called you 09:59

1hr 24mins

Thursday, 09 April 2020 11:26

chag sameach😃

Stephennnn 👍 this message 11:48

ty!! stay safe 😊

You 👍 this message 11:51

Saturday 18 April 2020 10:00

Stephennnn video called you 10:00

58mins

Thursday, 30 April 2020 08:31

Stephennnn video called you 08:31

22mins

Sunday 03 May 2020 10:02

Stephennnn video called you 10:02

51mins

Sunday 17 May 2020 10:00

Stephennnn video called you 10:00

55mins

Tuesday, 30 June 2020 08:29

readyyyyy♡

Stephennnn video called you 08:31

28mins

Sunday, 19 July 2020 10:02

Stephennnn video called you 10:02

1hr 18mins

Sunday, 30 August 2020 09:59

ready😇

Stephennnn video called you 10:00

1hr 06mins

Saturday, 07 November 2020 08:42

CONGRATULATIONS☑☑

Stephennnn video called you 09:13

18mins

Friday, 11 December 2020 12:06

chag sameach😃

Stephennnn 👍 this message 13:37

ty 😊!! and sorry can't

do this weekend

got my dates confused

next weekend ok?

You 👍 this message 13:39

See you next weekend😇

Today 09:59

Ready👀

Stephennnn video called you 10:01

42mins

Part 33

Nah Bruh, When You Search, You Gotta Add "Band"

A dream. A memory. Who can say which is more real.

Stephen was there. Time slowing. Mind taking a thousand photos a second.

Sweat. Bodies. Encased in sound.

Screaming his lungs out. Anger. Grief. Kinship.

He's not the only one who hurts like this. There are so many others. And some of them are right here. Moving like the sea. Swimming in the music. It doesn't matter who he is or who he's been. Not here.

Even as the time passes, and the moment becomes distant, hard to reach for, fading at the edges, crumpling under the weight of new, powerful, harrowing memories, it still was.

It will never truly fade. He will forever be jumping, singing, glistening in the lights, lost among the bodies, in the Philly Fillmore.

Hanging onto live music in the dying days, one last hit before the end of the world.

For him, there is truly no paradise, but the one we create.

We come together to celebrate, to share, to mourn. All in a dying effort to know that we are all here, in the now, never as aged, never as youthful, truly present in the company of others.

To be seen, to bear witness, to proclaim with words, with actions, with locked eyes, that we breathe in time, and we travel through snapshots, hoping to cling onto each other on the journey.

So many times, from phones, from sound systems, from car stereos, he's sung these lyrics, drummed on kitchen counter tops, shed tears, all to The Wonder Years.

Singing along as he unpacks in the company apartment, no idea what awaits him here in Melbourne, simply a person, putting away fabric and warmth, they were there.

Fingers tapping his kitchen island, as he waits for Lucas to get there, excited to see those rosy cheeks and plump lips, hear that Midlands accent, share an evening with that soul, they were there.

The oceans of sorrow spilling down his cheeks, as he sits alone on the tile floor of his kitchen, trying to process the news of returning home, they were there.

It's all here, and yet it's all gone.

For of course there's a before, there's an after, but right here, there is only now.

With the pounding drums, roaring guitars, and belting vocals, all carrying lyrics that seep into his skin, run along his bones, bury themselves deep in his heart, saying one simple truth: you are not alone.

Part 34

Saved To Notes

08/06/19 22:52

Ste. I don't even know how to day these things. I don't even know if they're real. I'm just destroyed. I'm barely a fraction of myself without you. Such a big part of me never wants to love someone like I loved you. I don't think I have the strength to this torn apart again. I want to never feel anything again

21/10/19 21:02

Fucking hell Ste it's like you spoke a language I'd never heard. And it was the most beautiful thing in the world. And I tried so hard to learn it. But just as I could get a few words out. You were gone. My glossary. gone instantly. I tried my whole life to never learn it. And you came swinging in with it. But I never wanna speak with anyone again.

04/01/20 01:28

If I could. I'd pull my heart right out of my chest. I'd move from this fucking apartment. And I'd live somewhere with no trace of you. I'd get another career. And talk to new people. Maybe get a new name. Be a new man. Maybe that would make me miss you less. Maybe I just need to get laid. Maybe I just need a new brain.

09/04/20 23:01

Right now I live in our past. I can't take the reality Ste.
So I remember all the times we had. It burns like fucking
nothing else. But at least it's not this. I don't think I'm
strong enough Ste. I can't do any of this without you. I'm
sorry I wasn't better. I'm sorry I didn't learn faster. And
fucking thank you for giving me a chance. And a million
more. You opened my heart. And I bleed from that
every fucking day.

27/05/20 21:56

I feel so fucking stupid. Did you see what I did? I said
feel not am. My therapist taught me that. She's the best.
Maybe if I marry her. I won't love you like this. I won't
fucking burn for you. The memories drown me Ste. I'm
fucking sinking. And there is no end. Only bottomless
fucking sea.

24/07/20 22:07

Ste I listened to that band you were always talking
about. It ripped through my fucking insides. But I felt so
understood. I get it. But I get you less. Maybe I never
knew you at all. The bluest things on earth tore my
fucking heart right out. Maybe I shouldn't have hoped
for that. That one line about wrapping arms around a
memory. If that isn't me with you right now. People who
say it's better to have loved and lost can fucking eat
shit. What I wouldn't give for a fucking drink and a
fucking line.

19/10/20 00:18

Ste I can't stop thinking about kissing you. Fuck you
were so good at it. Always had me feeling fucking sexy
and wanted. But now I feel like the ugliest worst thing on

the planet. I have a session w tomorrow. Maybe Dawn
will say something to make me feel less shit.

25/12/20 02:41

Fuck you're in my skin. Do you know that Ste? I can't
tell you how often I think about you to cum. Sometimes I
can't until I do. I'll be so close. But you push me over. I
know it's not romatic. Nothing to write poetry about. But
it's real. My body knows you too well.

16/01/21 03:14

Ste.. I'm sorry> I' stupid and I miss you" and I love you..
I'm drnk as fuck an everthling s clear to my finully../
fuck,, fuking elven yeass dw"wn the drain, bu?t it
is.."what it is I guess?....fukk stepen I cat stop thking
abot you,,but what els is fukkin new..

Part 35

I'm Indifferent Towards Emails!

From: Stephen Herzig <saherzig@outlook.com>
To: Lucas Watterson <lwatts80@gmail.co.uk>
Subject:

Hi Lu
I feel like we had a sorta weird call. I wanted to make it clear that though my feelings have changed over time. To me it doesn't take anything away from the time we spent together.

I sorta think we were like same-same but different. In this vacuum. It just sorta fell into place. Am I making sense?

I don't know how things might have been different if I'd stayed.

And I didn't say that stuff about practicing again to make you feel like I'd side-lined my identity for you.

It was a weird time, and you were this reprieve among it all. I do that a lot. I don't know if this makes sense. I don't know a lot I guess.

Saved to Drafts - 8:14PM Monday, December 20, 2020

Dear Reader

Thank you for purchasing, and reading, '*Where The Pink Meets The Blue*', and if you're skipping to the end, please go back and read it first. I promise you can come back to this letter once you've finished the story.

But we can never read a story for the first time again, so savour the unknown, and read it unspoiled if you can.

So, you've finished the story of Lucas Watterson and Stephen Herzig, two characters I love very much.

I hope you felt with these two, maybe cried with them, and enjoyed the journey.

I love to create love stories that don't end with a Happily Ever After, because to me, that isn't as true, or as relatable, as ones filled with questions, laced with regrets, and resulting in growth.

To me, most romances end, and this isn't something that scares me, it's something that intrigues me as a writer, and brings me a beautiful bittersweetness as a human.

Perhaps I'm setting myself up for reader backlash or long-term commercial failure, but I genuinely want to write stories that are grounded, that are human, and that have a stinging truth to them all.

I seek to reflect that pain is important, that love is a renewable resource, and that breakups and breakdowns alike don't have to mean the halting of progress.

Thank you for reading, and inviting my words into your life. I appreciate it very much.

Kind regards,

Neptune Henriksen

About The Author

Neptune Henriksen is a critically acclaimed writer and theatre maker, as well as an award-winning director.

Their works explore identity, sexuality, and emotional turmoil through a queer, intersectional lens, with love, humour, and introspection.

Their art is prolific and varied, from storytelling to comedy directing, microfiction to physical theatre, with their artistic voice always shining through, unique and clear.

Their works seek to comfort, to explore, and to shed light on topics often shied away from.

Other Works By The Author

Queer Summer Trilogy, 2022
Three novellas exploring queerness in the Australian Summer.

1. *'Where The Pink Meets The Blue'*, a bisexual erotica

2. *'Under A Summer Sky In January'*, a sapphic teen love triangle

3. *'We Used To Hold Hands All The Time'*, A romance of childhood friends reunited

'Daydreamings: A Collection Of Connections', 2020
A flash fiction collection, snapshots of moments of connection and relationships of all intersections.